Lily Tinsley

In the Ring

A novel. Part 3

Lily Tinsley

In the Ring
A novel. Part 3

ISBN/EAN: 9783337045807

Printed in Europe, USA, Canada, Australia, Japan

Cover: Foto ©Andreas Hilbeck / pixelio.de

More available books at **www.hansebooks.com**

BY

LILY TINSLEY,

AUTHOR OF "A WOMAN'S REVENGE," "THE WRECKER'S DAUGHTER,"
"THE LION QUEEN," "SHADOWS," "AT THE CROSS ROADS."

IN THREE VOLUMES.

VOL. III.

LONDON: TINSLEY BROTHERS,
8 CATHERINE STREET, STRAND.

———

1886.

COLSTON AND COMPANY, PRINTERS, EDINBURGH.

CONTENTS.

IN THE RING.

CHAPTER I.

A TALE OF SORROW AND PAIN.

To Jerry the tale told by Lizette in the calm weary voice which made the recital doubly real was every word new, but there is no occasion for me to repeat it. My reader already knows what happened on that night when, before the eyes of the terrified audience, the Fay of Fire missed her footing and fell, causing Bonfire to stumble also, just as he took his last leap. It was a terrible moment—horse and rider had rolled over together, the one entangled in the burning hurdle, the other stricken and helpless, at the mercy of those strong limbs which struck out so fiercely to regain a footing, and the hot, scorching flames which rose from the gate which but a moment before Carl Hermann, in obedience to a command of his wife's father, had been supporting.

No wonder the people turned pale, screamed and fainted—it was truly a sight to make the bravest heart sick with terror.

Brave hearts! There were no doubt many near who would willingly have stood up before any woman's enemy had he been ever so strong ; but who knew what help to give or how to act in such a case as this?

Every one stands still, staring either appealingly at his neighbour to know what to do, or turning away in very horror from the sight of that terrified animal plunging and kicking amidst the flames, which are beginning to burn even more fiercely where one catches sight of a scrap of something scarlet and the gleam of a shining helmet. Yes, every one waits for the other to make a move ; even the false-hearted lover for once stands out in his true character as a shrinking, trembling coward, until suddenly some one, who has made no soft-worded vows of love and homage—who does not even rank as the equal of a lad of but a few years old in common sense, finds love enough and wits enough to go to the rescue.

With strength of which no one looking at his shrunken form would have deemed him capable, he tears from the centre pole, to which they are attached, the long festoons of roses over which the Fay has so lately danced, and which he knows are fastened upon ropes of a considerable thickness.

"Come on!" he shouts excitedly, pushing his

way madly into the ring before the moment of waiting is quite over.

Although he utters no more explicit direction than this, his movement is the key for others who are quite as willing if not so quick as he is, and in less time than it takes to write, the long ropes of flowers are bound round Bonfire, so that he can kick and struggle no longer, and by many willing hands he is dragged out of the reach of the flames. These burst forth with renewed brightness round the motionless figure which is left to them, but heavy feet trample them out, and eager hands snatch away the burning masses of wood, and a heavy banner ends its work upon the scarlet dress, which it would burn to ashes, and its wearer too, if it had a chance.

Its wearer? Is that, then, a living being which lies so still upon the ground, in the centre of the throng? Living? Who can say? only the men are very, very gentle as they lift the hurdle upon which they have placed it; and have very white faces and trembling hands when they bear their burden out of sight within those heavy velvet curtains, which parted but a few moments before to give entrance to the fairy form of the Fay of Fire and her clever steed Bonfire. Where are they now?

It is all very well for the manager, bland and smiling, to step forth a few moments later and tell the people any amount of lies; so long as their minds are made easy, what does it matter? What if, later on in the night, there comes a sound of a gun-shot from the direction of the circus stables, which is poor Bonfire's death-warrant; while from that hour, in that dreary room in Wicker's Row, a bitter struggle between life, which is so full of anguish, and death, which is cruel enough to keep away, has commenced, and seems to have no hope.

The morning after her accident saw Lizette suffering not only from the injuries she had then sustained, which were in themselves of the gravest nature, but paying what in any case must have been the penalty of the struggle of the last few weeks, in a severe attack of brain fever.

The fight had been one such as few have to go through in their lives, and it was a marvel to those around her how one seemingly so frail as the little German girl could have come off victorious.

For many days her life was despaired of, but it seemed that the prayer she had so often prayed lately was not to be granted. Death, though he came near enough to cast the shadow of his wings over her, passed on elsewhere without folding them round her.

Her recovery, or rather escape, was perhaps all the more wonderful when the circumstances of it were remembered. Lizette's lodging was naturally a poor one; but when, after the accident, it was debated by those who had undertaken the merciful task, where they should take her, it was decided that as the hospital—which was undoubtedly the place where she should have gone—was such a long distance away, right at the other end of the town, it would be best to take her "home," or at least to the place she called home for the time, little as it deserved the name.

To Wicker's Row, therefore, up into that room against the sky, they carried all that was left of the little Fay of Fire. Here came the doctor to see her, a busy, practical man, who first seconded all Mrs Spicer's indignant protests that for such a case the hospital was the best place; but by-and-by, after a close examination, was of the opinion that of neither her room in Wicker's Row or at any hospital would his patient be long an inmate, the nature of her injuries was so severe that it hardly seemed possible that she could survive that night. But the morning came, and proved the doctor's calculation to be incorrect; that day and the following passed, seeing the fever which held her in a fiery hand still increasing ; morning grew to evening, evening to morning, many times, and still there was life, if little hope.

So it had gone on, till at length the turning-point was reached when it must be either life or death. And, although there was no one in all the world to offer up a petition that it might be "life," though if it had been "death" no one in that great city would have so much as missed the fair young life that had passed from out their midst, yet "life" was the heavier in the scale, and Lizette struggled back to life again. But, alas ! what a different life to the one that had once been.

In the search which had necessarily been made
of her belongings, fortunately for Lizette in the
presence of the doctor, the landlady had discovered a purse containing five sovereigns sewn
up in the body of her dress. Banking, for one
who led a wandering life, and might want her
little store at any moment, was, of course, out of
the question; indeed, was an unheard of thing
among the brotherhood, save, perhaps, in the case
of Jerry, who had managed to scrape together a
neat little sum prior to his illness, which he had
secretly deposited in the Post Office Savings Bank
till any time he should find a use for it.

This five pounds, however, was all that Lizette
had been able to save, with all her care, for the
day when it rained ; and fortunate it was for her
that she had done so, for the day which now
dawned was without doubt stormier and darker
than any even she in her care for the future had
imagined.

Its existence, to begin with, somewhat mollified
Mrs Spicer, who, on learning how grave was the
nature of her lodger's illness, was inclined to re-
sent it in a way peculiar to landladies.

She declared that she would undertake none of
the responsibilities of the affair, she had no one in
the house who could be spared to take the post of
nurse ; while as to the amount of work which
would necessarily be entailed, she did not at all
see how it was to be managed. And supposing
the girl were to die, a nice thing it'd be to have a
funeral from the house. Why, every one of her

lodgers would insist upon it that it was some infectious disease, that the drains were bad, or find some other reasons for vacating their quarters as quickly as possible ; to say nothing of who was going to pay the expenses of nursing and the burying—if it came to that.

The good woman ran on at some length in this strain, at every sentence gathering fresh indignation. 'Twas only by sheer strength of lung that the doctor at length reduced her to silence.

She swore (literally) that not another moment should Lizette stay in the house—the hospital was the place for her—whether she lived or died there wouldn't matter to nobody ; the lodgers there wouldn't hurry to be off any more, no matter what she did. Of that, at any rate, she (Mrs Spicer) was determined—to the hospital the sick girl should go.

On this point she insisted with such violence that nothing short of the doctor's threatening her with legal proceedings if she in any way disturbed his patient, would reduce her to order.

At this threat she was somewhat cowed, but even then I doubt if it would not have gone hardly with Lizette if the results of the search of her room had not been so satisfactory.

The discovery of the five pounds seemed to restore her temper a little ; but noting the way in which her watery grey eyes glistened as she counted the money in her hand, the doctor thought best to put in a claim to a direction of he fund.

At first milady was very loath to part with the coins; but being somewhat afraid of the doctor, who before now had shown that he was not to be put down even by the grimmest of landladies, she at length handed him the neat little sum.

She paid him out, however, in more ways than one, as is the practice of the tribe; but that is a matter of no importance, since but for him Lizette must have suffered severely.

On being asked the sum she had agreed to let the room to the fancy-rider for a week, she named exactly double that which she had in reality demanded; but, knowing he had no power to contradict her, the doctor paid over to her rent for the said room for six weeks to come, making her sign a proper receipt for the same, thus securing his patient undisputed possession of the top-front until she should be able to act for herself.

His next step was to procure a nurse, an expense which would have been spared, and indeed many comforts besides been Lizette's had she been taken to the hospital; but since it was too late for the removal, he (the doctor) was bound to do what he could.

And well was it for Lizette that she had such a conscientious friend in her physician. One almost wonders how, with so much work to do in the big city, the hard-working man had time to spare for any duties but those which his profession demanded. But, though to all appearances a bluff, almost rough, practical man, there was a soft corner in his heart which was touched by the friendless stranger's helplessness.

He himself made some inquiries at the show, and since Lizette's engagement was not up, quietly informed Mr Petman that her salary would of course be paid as usual up till the time agreed for her dismissal.

This, of course, though he blustered and protested a good bit, the manager could not gainsay; and fearful, perhaps, lest by-and-by, if he refused, Lizette might lay damages against him to no small amount, he paid down the sum at once. This added to the scanty store, which was yet terribly small when one thinks of the great battle which it was to help to fight.

So all things were made ready, and for days and days the struggle went on; then came the turning-point, and after that the slow coming back to life.

This last was the hardest work of all. Lizette might certainly have been said to conquer, but as yet she was by no means master of her kingdom; and while rejoicing in the skill which had triumphed when defeat seemed more than possible, Dr Woodward was baffled, perplexed, and not a little chagrined at his patient's very slow recovery.

He was a clever man, no doubt, but, in his study of the body, he was apt to forget that the healing of the mind is a far more difficult task.

It did occur to him, however, one day that there was something more the matter here than his learning could grapple with.

It was the day after he had dismissed the nurse, for the money had nearly all gone, only enough left to keep the girl alive, even if she lived in the plainest way. Even then he had had to leave his own fee entirely out of the question, which is a hard thing for a man with a sickly wife and a family of growing children to do. It was not the first time Dr Woodward had practised this sort of charity, and he had so far never lost by it, as indeed it was impossible he should. It was, I say, on the day he had dismissed Mrs Seton, the motherly woman who had been such a conscientious nurse during the time of the fever, that the doctor, during his visit, spoke in his usual blunt way to Lizette of her affairs, questioning her as to how she meant to live in the future, and many other kindly-meant inquiries; to all of which the invalid answered fretfully, " She didn't know," evincing such perfect unconcern as to the future that the physician deemed it best to acquaint her with the true state of affairs.

Lizette listened with her usual weary langour at first, but when she at length roused herself to comprehend the true state of affairs, it was pitiful to see her helplessness and despair.

" Why could she not go back to her old work? " she asked, almost fiercely.

The doctor's answer was to bid her walk across the room. With a flush of excitement which told of a powerful effort of will, she dragged herself up from the couch where she lay, and went to do his bidding. But, alas! she over-calculated her strength; scarcely had she taken half-a-dozen steps than there came that dull pain in her back she had felt so often before, the room seemed to swim round her; she staggered, and only saved herself from falling by catching hold of a chair. This experiment at least was a sufficient answer to her question, but it lead to a far more dangerous one—one which the doctor had long dreaded.

Hitherto Lizette had, as I have said, evinced not the slightest interest in life whatever; one would almost have imagined, from the utter unconcern she had about everything that has triumphed over death, she was content merely to live in the sense of breathing, and nothing more. Now she suddenly sat up on the battered old sofa, which Mrs Spicer, by dint of bribery, had been induced to add to the scanty furniture of the room, pushed her hair back off her forehead, seeming to note for the first time that it was not half so abundant as before she had been taken ill, passed her hands wonderingly across her face, and then looking up suddenly, said, "Am I different—since I have been ill, I mean? You said I had a scar—a scar—what is it? Is it—with a sudden strange look in her eyes as she scanned the doctor's countenance— "is it something that will show—a mark—is it?"

And again her hands travelled over her features with nervous eagerness.

Off his guard by the action and tone, a pitying

look crept into the doctor's eyes, and in a moment Lizette read its meaning.

She sprang to her feet with a startled cry, holding out her hands with that peculiar gesture of entreaty which had so often charmed Jerry.

"It is a scar. I can feel it, and I can see by your face I am different. Oh, let me see, please let me see."

Long since, on some trivial pretence, the doctor had hidden away an old cracked looking-glass which hung on the wall over the make-shift for a dressing-table, but now he knew it was time the glass should be brought from its hiding-place. Hesitation would mean suspense to the girl, and who could not guess how painful that would be?

"Look at yourself? Of course you can. There's a sure sign you'll be yourself soon when the vanity begins to show itself. I had a patient once who, when she was dying, let go her husband's hand to put her hair straight, and died with a curl twisted round her finger. Just like women, they always," etc. So the doctor ran on, while he made a pretence of looking for something, which he knew very well was close at hand, trying hard to make himself out a veritable woman-hater because of the vanity of the softer sex; but when he found the mirror under a pile of rubbish in the corner, where no one would have dreamt of looking save he who put it there, why did he make a great show of rubbing up its surface by breathing on it and rubbing it with his sleeve, or rather making a pretence to do the latter, for when he at length

held out the glass to Lizette, it was still dull with
his breath.

Now he said, very gruffly even for him, " It's no
use your trying to recognise your likeness in such
a glass as this; it might as well be a piece of
block tin ; besides, your imprisonment in this hole
isn't calculated to bring roses to your cheeks,
and—"

" I know, I know " interrupted Lizette, almost
snatching away the glass, and turning to the light
with a feverish eagerness which was almost painful.   A moment she bent over it, then it fell from
her hands to the floor with a hollow sound as it
rattled in its wooden frame, and, with a cry of
pain, like that of a wounded animal, she hid her
face in the cushions on the couch.

The doctor had seen such a scene often before,
had stood by while strong men had bemoaned the
cruel fate which had made them henceforth feel as
though they must shun the gaze of their fellow-
creatures, had heard their cries of resentfulness ;
but there was something so indescribably pitiful
in this mute agony that he had no words of any
sort at his command.

He waited till presently it seemed to him he
could not break the silence.   This was no sickness
such as he could heal, so stole silently, noiselessly,
out of the room and down the creaking stairs.
At the foot of the stairs the doctor met Sarah,
as usual laden with brooms, dust-pans, and boxes,
and such like implements of torture for cleaning.
Evidently there was something in his face which

was unusual, for she came to a dead standstill in front of him, essayed to express her astonishment, as was her usual habit, by clasping her hands, an endeavour which resulted in the downfall of several of the said implements with a clatter to the ground, as she said, in an awe-struck whisper, " Lor', sir, whatever is it ? "

" What's what ? " asked the doctor, with a fierceness which was fatal to the rest of the brooms—" what's what ? "

" Why, you're a-looking—oh, just awful—as if you'd seen, oh, I don't know what." Sarah's modes of expression were not very intelligible sometimes. " She ain't worse, is she ? Oh, lor', I do hope she ain't. She drank some of that broth I made her, unbeknown to missus ; perhaps it ain't agreed with her ; perhaps it was too strong."

The said broth had been inspected and tasted by the doctor, who had pronounced it to be the most magnificent compound of colouring and warm water he had ever tasted, but the fact of it having been made by Sarah's hands—I can hardly call them fair—gave him a sudden idea.

If ever a girl was in want of a friend, it was the little German rider, crying her eyes out because of the sad tale the looking-glass told. This big, stolid slavey he had often, when coming to pay his visits, found lingering outside the top single front door, always shuffling away at his approach, sometimes have some business in the hall at his departure, and pausing to ask, in her shame-faced way, " How do you think she is up there?" as though possessed of the idea that his visit had made some material change in his patient.

Hitherto, however, it would appear that the presence of the nurse had had an overawing effect upon the girl, for the moment the house had been freed of her, this clumsy, awkward creature had made offers of help on behalf of the invalid.

The episode of the broth had made the physician feel somewhat sarcastically inclined towards the maker, but now, in the girl's unconscious earnestness, he fancied he recognised a kindly soul beneath the not very prepossessing exterior.

Some people might have laughed at the idea of a friendship between little Lizette and this queer girl, but Dr Woodward knew it was no time to pick and choose, even if by a more studied selection his choice would have been more beneficial to those concerned.

Lizette wanted a friend—here was one close at hand, who, if circumstances told truly, was only too ready and willing to fill the office.

How, when there were so many steps between her dominion below and that of the invalid up in the sky, she had been daily aware of anything more than the top-front lodger's existence, was a mystery he did not stay to solve.

He only coughed meditatively once or twice while buttoning up his coat—uncertain how to act—whether to tell Sarah of the thoughts he had in his mind, or to drop a word of meaning and leave it to work as it might.

Remembrance of the many times she had so

often shuffled out of his way, as though ashamed of having betrayed any interest, however, decided him.

"How is it," he said suddenly, looking across into her face, "that I so often find you at work on the stairs when I come? You're up to no good, I'll be bound, wasting your time. I hope you're not waiting for an opportunity to make something out of that poor little thing upstairs— because I've got my eyes open."

At this accusation, which might have staggered a far more unscrupulous soul than Sarah, the girl only pushed her hair back off her face with a look of stolid defiance, which was more intelligible than her protest.

"You can think what you likes; I knows better this once."

The girl was so used to being attacked on the score of her honesty, and not without cause, for she had been picked up from the gutter by her present mistress—herself no very choice specimen of humanity—that there was no mistaking the pride with which she, for once, rested on the fact of her innocence.

Dr Woodward was not slow to perceive this, and changed his tactics accordingly.

"There," he said, appealing to an imaginary audience, "that's always the way with you girls; never will own you've got a kindly thought about anybody; try to make yourselves out as bad as— as your mistresses. I wonder you aren't ashamed of yourselves. Where's the harm, I should like to know, if you, Jane—not Sarah—isn't it, do feel as if you'd like to help one of your fellow-creatures a bit? Don't she want it bad enough? I've done all I can, but I can't do more; as it is, I ought to be in a dozen different places this minute, and I've got to leave this girl now to get on as best she can. I know it sounds hard—so it is—when a man spends his health and strength in bringing a poor soul back from the grave, he must be a brute beast if, as soon as she's got enough life in her to know what it is she's suffering and got to suffer, he doesn't feel as if that poor creature, if she hasn't got any one else, somehow belongs to him. 'Tisn't often it happens—most folks have somebody to care for them and see after them a bit, but this girl hasn't—not a single one. At the show when I went there wasn't one as could say much, for fear, I believe, of the master, but they'd their duties—just as I have mine—and so this girl has to struggle on alone as best she can. Lord! I've tried to do my duty by her, but perhaps it'd been kinder to let her go. Death's mighty easy work when one looks at it beside what we have to go through in life. But there, I mustn't talk of dying, though after all it mayn't be long she's got to trouble even to live. What I think of is, how she is going to get on at all alone up there. She's only a child, and this work has pulled her down awfully. If she'd only some one who'd help her to bear it a bit; even if Mrs Spicer'd give her a hand like she did you when you were just as put about—not but what you've

paid for her bit of trouble by this time—it might
be the saving of her, body and soul. If only any
one 'd be willing — it isn't half as hard work as
being a general servant, though the pay's different.
If any one 'd be willing and help her to bear it,
it 'd be worth all the medicine put together that
I could give her."

The doctor paused, drawing on his gloves with
great precision ; Sarah stood dusting the bannisters with her greasy apron, and scraping the
wooden stair with the toe of her ragged boot in a
way which put her listener's teeth on edge.

" Ain't there nobody as 'd do—leastways 'd try
for a bit ? " she asked abruptly.

" Well," returned the doctor, smiling down most
benignly at a refractory button of his glove,
" there is some one, but she's got so much to do
already, I don't like to impose upon her kindness."

This last sentence told visibly upon Sarah. She
left off dusting, but scraped with renewed vigour,
till the doctor's nerves fairly danced in his body in
a manner totally unbefitting those of a well-bred
respectable surgeon.

" Do I know who it is ? " she asked, even more
abruptly.

" Who ? This somebody I alluded to ? Oh,
yes ; she's a friend of yours."

" I ain't got no friends," said Sarah, her face
falling suddenly, her dull brain failing to take in
the doctor's meaning.

" Yes, you have," returned the doctor, with much
assurance ; " and this friend of yours is just the

sort of friend wanted up there," with a motion towards his patient's room above.

"But supposing she"—also with a motion in that direction — "supposing she don't like it. 'Tain't always the ladies as can afford to rent the parlours. Afore she was took ill I seed her going in and out sometimes, and if any one 'd ask me where I'd have put her, it wouldn't have been a step higher than the first-floor front."

Taking this figurative language to mean that it was a sense of being her inferior by the (again figuratively speaking) unlimited distance which intervenes between the upper and lower regions of the house, which was the reason of Sarah's uneasiness, Dr Woodward was somewhat in a dilemma how to smooth away the difficulty.

Like a wise man, he decided to let it alone ; aware, too, that he had already wasted far more time on this mission than he could really afford, he planted his well-worn beaver over his bald head, and said, in his most business-like manner, " Just as if it matters when folks are in trouble, whether they live in the kitchen or in the drawing-room. All I know is, this girl wants some one to help her to bear this trouble, and there's some one could do it if she liked."

Without another word he hastened down the stairs, and banged the door behind him.

For some moments after he had turned the end of the street, and had forgotten his late argument in a far more important one, in which he was trying to decide whether it would be better for a certain burly carpenter among his patients to hop through life on one leg, or run the risk of in a short time departing for the next one with one whole and one battered one, the "slavey" stood industriously completing the destruction of her boots by scraping them alternately on the stairs.

In this interesting operation she was disturbed by the usual dispeller of both her waking and sleeping dreams, the shrill call of "Sarah! Sarah!" followed by the usual running accompaniment of angry grumblings. Obedient to this admonition, the girl collected one by one, with her usual slowness of movement, her brooms and brushes, and knocking their several handles against the bannisters at every step, which roused in the minds of several of Mrs Spicer's lodgers the idea that for their special torment their landlady had hired some one to perform a clog dance on the stairs, she slowly returned to her work.

Her interview with the doctor had taken place late in the morning, and it was not till late in the afternoon that, on any pretext whatever, she could make her escape from the lower realms and ascend to those above.

When, however, she did so, any one to have watched her stealing as quietly as her ungainly body would let her, up the stairs—pausing now and then to make sure that no enemy was aware of her movements—might easily have believed that the doctor's lately uttered suspicions were not unfounded.

Up she went, doing her very utmost to avoid a noise, but even then not escaping more than one violent collision with one or two objects which came in her way, until at length she reached the door leading into the sick chamber, at which, drawn as the strong and healthy sometimes are by an irresistible impulse to inquire after the welfare of those who had so lately been like ourselves, she had so often lingered. Even now, after her timid knock had been answered by a low "Come in," she paused and drew back timidly more than once before apparently she could screw up enough courage to take the final step—namely, into the room.

At length, however, she pushed open the door, knocking her elbows against it and the post, and entered.

During her ascent she had held with much care the corners of her coarse apron in one hand, as though it contained something precious, seemingly in the shape of a ball, which rolled about from corner to corner at each of her bungling movements, while from time to time a faint squeak made itself heard.

Having entered the room, Sarah stood for at least five minutes, blinking and winking in the darkness like a great big owl.

When her eyes had got used to the darkness she saw Lizette lying in almost the same attitude as when the doctor had left her, crying no longer, but sitting looking with red swollen eyes out of the window.

"Is that you, Mrs Spicer?" she asked, hardly troubling to turn her head.

"No; 'tain't the missus; it's me."

Even the fact of having such an unexpected visitor did not rouse her curiosity. Without evincing the slightest interest she waited for what was to come next, apparently totally indifferent to what it was.

This reception was certainly a very chilling one, and every moment that flew by saw Sarah getting more and more confused and uncertain what to do. How heartily did she wish she had never been induced to undertake the mission— that she was back again in the region of pots and pans.

Whatever was she to say or do? After repeating this question over and over again to herself with such energy that she gave herself no time for a reply, at last she made a step forward. This movement did not mend matters, for not, of course, troubling to look where she was going, she planted her foot right in the centre of the mirror, which still lay on the ground, with a natural result that she, being by no means fairy in form or weight, the glass was smashed to, if not the proverbial thousand pieces, yet quite sufficient to render it fit only for the dustbin.

"Oh, lor'," said Sarah, ruefully regarding the shattered fragments, "I've done it this time," not intending to imply that she had attempted the destruction of the said glass on any former occasion, but merely that the mishap was quite in accordance with her luck.

The movement of despair which accompanied this assertion was so violent that a more than usually loud and prolonged squeal made itself heard from the depth of her apron.

This endued her with an idea.

Without more ado she plunged both her hands in among the said apron's greasy folds, from whence she produced what appeared to be a roll of dirty-looking white wool.

This she regarded with great amusement, then making another step forward, less disastrous than the first, poked it with great energy into Lizette's lap.

"I thought you might like to see one of the cat's new kittens. Don't keep it if you don't want to, but the doctor said you was lonely like, so I thought it might be a bit of company."

Before she could say more, the never-failing cry of "Sarah! Sarah!" made itself heard, and for once not sorry for its interruption, she turned and retreated backwards out of the room, and, evidently to atone for her care in her journey up, made a doubly noisy descent, reaching the kitchen with a memento of her errand in the shape of a zig-zag tear in her apron, and a still more lasting one—a big black bruise on her forehead, which, in her precipitous retreat, had come in contact with the corner of the hat-stand in the hall.

Meanwhile, in the room near the sky, Lizette

had been a little frightened at first to find the ball in her lap was alive. She tried to shake it on to the floor, but it clung to her hand, flew up her sleeve, and nestled in her neck, and before she quite knew how, there was a soft, furry little kitten, with the biggest of blue eyes, whirring and purring in an infantine, spasmodic way under her chin.

Who could resist such a messenger of comfort? Certainly not poor full-hearted little Lizette.

Although the tears did not come, there was a breach made in the barrier of iron which was round her heart, as, clasping her hands over the funny little ball of wool, she hid her face in it, the face which had so startled her when she had seen it in the glass, and somehow felt as if the world and life was not so dreary after all.

Later on in the day, when Sarah made her escape once more, and went bungling into the room, she found the sick girl with the kitten curled up on her lap, while she languidly turned over the bag which contained some of her belongings.

She did not, however, seem inclined to talk, for silence with her was such a habit it was hard to get out of it, so Sarah set to work with unnecessary energy to sweep up the remains of the glass, making an abnormal amount of noise and dust in the operation.

This done, she stood with her arms akimbo, regarding the invalid and the kitten with great stolidity.

" You'll keep her, I suppose," she said suddenly, alluding, of course, to the latter.

" Yes," said Lizette, awakening to the fact that she must say something. " Yes, please. It was good of you to bring her for me."

" Lor' bless you, I'd have saved the whole lot if I'd have known it'd please you. There was four of them. Missus, when she found 'em in the clothes basket, said, ' Take 'em down and drown 'em,' but I thought as how maybe you'd like one, so I saved the littlest. It's a mercy I didn't kill it bringing it up, things do get in the way so. But there, they say cats has got nine lives— though it do seem strange such a ' weeny ' thing should have such a lot, and us folks only one. It is a ' weeny ' thing, isn't it ? "

Whatever might be the literal meaning of this adjective, Lizette did not attempt to dispute the fact, but roused herself sufficiently to offer her thanks for the service. And with a few more remarks of a like nature to those usually volunteered by the servant girl, the interview ended.

But unpromising as it had been, the acquaintance thus commenced from that time certainly progressed.

Naturally, considering the circumstances, it was hardly likely any startling manifestation of friendship should be made. Lizette, though she hugged the kitten to her and whispered her sorrows into its funny little ears, was too tightly held by that iron band round her heart to make any great sign, and Sarah's time was never really her own ;

it was only by stealing a few moments now and then that she was able to introduce her big figure into the dreary little attic, where, more often than not, before she had got over the fit of shyness which for some seconds after her entrance kept her staring at the sick girl as though she had been some sort of natural curiosity, there would come that call of "Sarah! Sarah!" and she would have to blunder down the stairs again without having uttered so much as one word.

But though their intercourse was of such a piecemeal nature, it was better than nothing, and if Sarah took more delight in the little offices she performed than did Lizette, at least the invalid's personal comfort was looked after, even if the healing of her mind, as the doctor had hoped, did not begin.

As we know, Sarah's intentions were better far than her actions. She had not even the power of saying coherently what she felt, and when we are in trouble we are too apt to think of what others might do for us, without calculating what little they in reality do.

A white kitten, too, is not a very substantial form of comfort, and in this case there was a dash of melancholy in the pleasure which Lizette took in the servant-girl's offering.

Not many days after it first came into her possession she discovered it was blind. The blue eyes, which she thought were so beautiful, had over them a white film, which, alas! made them pretty to see not to see with.

On making the discovery, Sarah had wished to award to the afflicted animal the same fate as that which she had bestowed upon its three unhappy brethren, wishing to supply its place with one of a large family lately presented by a tabby to a near neigbour.

To this, however, Lizette would not consent.

It might have been that her love for the poor little beast had sprung up the moment it had been poked into her lap on that memorable day, but I think there was a queer fancy in her heart that made her cling to it all the more because it was denied the use of its eyes, and, therefore, could never know what its mistress was like.

Poor foolish child! little did she know how often brute beasts are more sagacious in their likings than human beings, never judging their masters or mistresses by their outer man.

Anyhow the "weeny" little thing was fairly installed in the top front attic as Lizette's pet and plaything.

But, as I have said, a kitten is not a very substantial form of comfort, and to the little German girl life seemed very dreary indeed,—as though she was without a friend near her,—as though it would have been far more kind of those who had tended her in her sickness to have let her die.

How many of us during our struggle in the world think the same, and yet we have all to live.

So Lizette found it. Her little store was so low, it seemed but a few shillings lay between her and beggary. These she eked out as best she could, but even while she prayed to die, she felt she must make some effort to keep body and soul together.

At first, as with many like her, the task seemed hopeless, then fortune favoured her in the shape of the projected wedding of the parlour lodger.

This lady, a widow of uncertain years, it so happened, needed a little help in some needle-work she had undertaken. By means of a stray word from Sarah, Lizette learnt this fact, and with as much eagerness as she evinced in anything now, offered her services.

Being quite a novice in such matters, she left the question of terms to the widow, who proved her claim to any amount of gratitude by naming half the sum any ordinary seamstress would have asked. Lizette, however, dared not refuse the straw held out, and so the days went by seeing her not growing one jot less frail or sickly, nay, even losing strength while she slaved with aching head and weary fingers for pay which she could once have easily earned by the light, easy work of a rider.

Early and late, early and late, with weary frame she carried on the outward struggle, early and late, whether she would or no, went on that other fearful struggle in her weary mind, the war-ring between good and evil.

Daily now that question, " Where will it end ? " was in her mind. Before it had only been in reference to weariness of soul, now the not more terribly but doubly pressing demand was on her, the wants and needs of her body. These must be attended to and striven for, and to one in Lizette's position the striving was doubly hard, for the reason that the very effort was not prompted by her own wish, because of that double weakness which had fallen so suddenly upon her.

And when one's will is not strong enough to pray for strength, because every moment brings its pain, there is little wonder that instead of rising step by step higher and higher we sink lower and lower.

It seemed to Lizette as if to any further depth she could not go. Utterly alone and friendless in the big city, suffering from a weakness which made every movement painful to her, grieving because of the remembrance of that strange, fearful face which had looked at her from out the mirror, her whole life seemed wrecked by the hope in which she had trusted so implicitly.

Poor little stranger, it was truly pitiful. How often when she sat alone in her bare, cheerless room would the thoughts rush in such a stream into her mind, that she would clench her fingers over her burning forehead to try and stay them. How often, when her head was bent over the work, which recalled wedding bells to her mind and the bright pictures of what might have been, the needle would be hidden from her sight by a dull mist over her eyes, and presently her face would be hidden in her thin white hands, through which the hot scalding tears would trickle slowly

down, and fall one by one on the soft ball of fur
curled up in her lap.

These tears came not in a great bursting torrent, such as would have calmed and refreshed
her, but in that slow rotation which told they
were wrung from a heart full to bursting.

Even the fountain of these was dried as time
wore on, and in its place came a new sensation
rather than a feeling strange and terrible.

Hitherto Lizette had looked upon her solitude
in that dreary little room near the sky as a heaven-
sent boon—a hiding-place, such as it was—just
what she felt in need of.

Now, however, as the time wore on, almost
without knowing how, a change came over her
ideas.

The hiding-place was such no longer, but a
prison in which her young life, which had once
been so bright, was to flicker and flicker, like a
burnt-out candle in its socket, till by-and-by, with
no one to know, no one to care, the feeble light
should die out altogether.

It is often the case that those who have longed
for death when they have been in the midst of life,
or, at any rate when, with some straw to hold on
to, have shrunk from it with fear and trembling
when they stand alone to face it.

Yes, that was the feeling with Lizette. When
the doctor had fought her battle for her she had
resisted; but now she was left with "no one
scarcely to know—no one to care," it all seemed
so fearful.

" No one to know — no one to care!" Over
and over again to herself she repeated the
thought, till by-and-by there came over her that
strange, awful feeling—that dread of being alone
—a sudden fear of her own thoughts—a hungry
longing for company—for some event to break the
dreadful monotony of never-ending moments—a
monotony which was like a grim dark shadow
which daily, hourly grew more impenetrable, more
dense, until it seemed it would close entirely
round her, and shut her in for ever from this world.

And then when the gloom was so great there
came a ray of hope like a broad sunbeam streaming
into a darkened room.

She heard a voice calling her back from the
terrors which were dragging her down, down,
she knew not where. She felt strong arms folding her shrunken form in their strong hold, and
an honest face looking down at her with eyes
that did not turn away from her because of the
little there was left to know her as her former
self, eyes which grew soft and tender with love and
pity.

CHAPTER II.

"I LOVED HIM SO."

AND so Jerry's long, weary search was at an end —yes, the search, but not the struggle.

What he had imagined would be the end of all his troubles, the finding of Lizette, was in reality a sudden darkening of the brightness of the future which he had planned for himself—a future in which he was to be content with knowing that she he loved was happy and well cared for.

How different was the actual fact. Lizette alone, friendless, not many steps from death's door, with scarcely strength to live in the present, shrinking fearfully from any thoughts of what was to come.

If ever a brave heart sickened, it was Jerry's, when he fully realised the greatness of the poor girl's desolation, and the fierce battle which she had been left to fight alone.

And all the while he had pictured her at least well in health, and with the means to live, praying in his inmost heart that the cruel burden which had been so suddenly laid upon her frail shoulders might one day be removed, and she become the happy, light-hearted girl he had once known her.

And while he was absent from her, bearing his part in the fight against unselfishness and disappointed hope as best he could, she, instead of traversing calmly the path which should lead to peace and joy once more, was sinking—sinking, slowly but surely, down the dark, yawning gulf of despair and helplessness.

We know that the young clown had been no laggard in his efforts to find her, but how often, when he found how much his coming was needed, did he reproach himself for even the little time he had dallied on his journey.

Every moment he had wasted had added one more to those of bitterest suffering which had already passed over the bowed head of her he loved.

Had he only known this, not day or night would he have rested until he was at her side—that was the thought which dimmed the tempered joy of the meeting ; and when he realised that perhaps even had he had wings wherewith to reach her he might have been too late, he felt a leaden weight fall upon his heart, so that he could scarce bring himself to release the slight form from his clasping arms, fearing lest, after all, his coming might be of little use to raise the drooping flower from where it had fallen among the dirt and ashes of bitterness and sorrow, and plant it once more in the sunlight of happiness and strength.

When Lizette at length drew herself away he

suddenly recalled his scattered senses, and, taking
a seat a little away from her, prepared to listen to
her story.

He would, perhaps, have preferred to have
waited a little before hearing it, to have had a
little time to recover himself; but he thought,
and rightly too, that it would be a relief to the
girl to tell some one her troubles ; and at present
so much was totally inexplicable to him that he
gave himself up to listen patiently.

So there in the darkened room the poor little
girl poured out her tale of sorrow. It was well
for Jerry that his face was, like everything else
in the room, in shadow, so that the expressions
which flitted across it were hidden from the brown
eyes which peered so wearily in his direction.

When the tale was finished he did not speak
for some minutes. How could he, with the big
lump in his throat, making it almost impossible
for him to keep from choking, while the tears were
slowly welling from his eyes and trickling down
his rough cheeks on to his yellow coat, one falling
on the beautiful crimson necktie and putting to
shame the bit of glass which served for a diamond
in the wonderful pin.

Presently, however, he managed to master his
agitation. Clearing his throat with a loud cough,
he muttered something about having a cold, which
he must have caught very quickly, as we know he
was in excellent condition when he entered the
room. This little farce over, he gave his necktie
a savage tug to restore it to ts right position,

performing the same act with such violence that he nearly strangled himself; ran his hands through his hair, thereby disturbing the excellent order to which it had been reduced by the application of several ounces of that far-famed pomatum known as "bear's grease," and smelling uncommonly like ordinary, or rather extraordinarily rank dripping; while, at the same time, from sheer force of habit he began whistling softly the tune, I think, of a favourite comic song of the day—hardly appropriate to the occasion, but exactly in accordance with his strange ways.

This, however, he soon cut short, and rising to his feet—he always said what he had got to say better when he was standing—also sheer force of habit, I suppose—began in his blundering way to try and convey the sympathy he felt.

Of course, he only succeeded in giving utterance to the most commonplace sentiments, such as sounded but cold and stiff in comparison to the pitiful tale he had so lately heard. But, you see, he wasn't a hero in a melodrama, with a marvellous amount of grand heroic sentences ready on his lips, in which to extol his own valour, his love for his lady-love, and his defiance of any ills, mortal or immaterial. He was merely an ordinary —I may say a very ordinary—young man, who, although gifted in public with a faculty for saying the right thing at the right moment, in private he was anything but ready with his tongue.

On this occasion, particularly, he was even more than usually reticent. I think the fact was that he had so many thoughts in his head that not one of them could find its way out.

If he had at that moment happened on a big boy teasing or in any way ill-treating a smaller one, I fancy it would have gone rather hard with the bully.

The relief which this outward expression of his feelings would have been to him was immense.

Unfortunately, however, he was alone in that dreary room without anything hitable near him, the consequence of which rush of subdued excitement to his brain—a matter of very unusual occurrence with him—was a species of mental paralysis at once dangerous and prejudicial to the cause in hand.

Although not usually by any means accounted a hard swearer, at that particular moment it would have been no little relief to him to have used some hard words against certain people and circumstances. But even this tiny safety valve was shut for him.

Somehow he could not let off the steam in this manner before Lizette. The illustration did not occur to him, but I verily believe he would as soon have thought of speaking of the place of everlasting darkness in the presence of an angel fresh from the realms of eternal day as of using any but polite language while that white wan face looked at him across the gloom.

Polite language meant with Jerry just the very most ordinary he could possibly use, and in such he expressed his sympathy with his little friend

—language which, I fear, was anything but calculated to pour balm on a wounded heart.

I make this confession because I do not wish
that troublesome person of the name of Jerry to
sail under false colours. I know the light in
which he appears to my reader is anything but
the rosy one to which his position in this story
entitles him, but I gave warning at the beginning
how it would be, so do not lay the fault at his
door, but at mine, if he falls short of pleasing.
Perhaps Lizette may appear to have been rather
open in her expressions of joy at his coming;
but when he had appeared so suddenly before
her, she had forgotten all else but that here at
last was some one who would befriend her in her
trouble.

In her greeting there had been no under-current
of feeling. She was glad to see him because he
was some one to help her. She would have
welcomed, I believe, any one with that quality
just as eagerly.

It was not until she felt his arms round her, his
lips brush her cheek, his voice calling her "Not to
be afraid, he was there, he would never leave her,
never forsake her," did she realise how truly she
had found help at last.

So fraught with consolation was the thought,
that she never stayed to put any second meaning
to the words.

Why should she?

To her it seemed that the lamp of love in her
life had completely gone out; she did not dream

that Jerry, her funny, awkward friend, should ever have thought of rekindling it.

To her he was a friend; she did not even then know that he was the very friend of all others she would most have cared to have come to her in her distress; she thought it was merely by some lucky chance that he had come and found her when she seemed lost for ever, had been so touched by the change in her that he had treated her as he would a sister, put his arms round her, cried with her, kissed her and spoken words of pity and comfort to her such as only a kind brotherly heart could have dictated.

It was but natural that she should take this view of the matter, for their relations prior to the entrance of the ring-master on to the scene had been of the simplest and most easy kind.

We know how he had taken the little stranger under his wing at first from pity, but how was she to tell how long since the pity had grown into the tenderer feeling?

He had never told her, and she was too occupied in the demolition of her own fairy castle to notice how high his was building.

She was too much of a child yet in the world's ways to know that it is not always those who say the most that mean the most. Even her late experience of how little truth a glib tongue can tell had not begun to bear its fruits.

Jerry need not have pulled himself up so short, for she was totally unaware of any material change in his manner, being only too contented to know that he was there, without entering into any question of why or wherefore. If afterwards she recalled to mind what had happened, it was not till then that she was aware that anything was amiss.

But if Jerry could not show his real feelings by words, he did so in a far better way, in deeds.

That evening, after he had left Lizette in her new frame of mind to look forward to a better and more restful night than formerly — hopes, however, doomed to be disappointed when he reached home, or rather what was then his home —he did not go to bed at once, but sat some time trying to map out a plan for the future.

Now that the momentary excitement of the meeting was over, there was no part of it so present to his mind as that cry which he had listened to in the darkness, the dreaming appeal to the absent lover whose faithlessness had not yet killed the love he had so wantonly flung away.

No matter how fervent had been her greeting to her friend who had found her in such sore trouble, above it all rose that soul-stirring entreaty to Carl to come back and to love her.

Try as he would, Jerry could not drown it in his ears. It struck the last blow to the hope in his heart. Beneath it the last cherished straw to which he had clung lay buried. Henceforth the light of his love, already dwindled down to such a tiny flame, had gone out.

Yes, but the lamp of friendship was still at hand, and never before had it needed trimming so much.

It seemed as if the task of this frail, helpless creature had been cast upon him to try the strength of his self-reliance. It remained to him whether he was faithful to his trust or no.

So, although he had resolutely declared this girl was "nothing to him," he nevertheless set about making what plans he could for her benefit.

Of one thing he was certain. She must not remain where she was. The very atmosphere of the attic was such as to destroy any likelihood of recovery.

She must be removed, and that at once, to a more healthy situation. This at least would be one step in the right direction.

Having settled this, he retired to rest, not I am bound to say to enjoy any better repose than did Lizette, for, for ever in his ears rang that cry, "Carl, Carl, I haf loved you so. I shall die if you do not love me." Late the following morning he paid Lizette a visit. Seeing her in the light of the morning was far different to doing so in the gloom of the evening before.

He could scarce keep himself from breaking out into the expressions of sympathy which he had suppressed the night before.

It was only because he knew how they would pain her that he was kept from so doing.

But the sight of her white wan face, so different from the rounded one he had last seen it, above all, that scar which told such a double tale of suffering. touched his rough heart till it was full to bursting. The wound had to all appearance been a fearful one, and showed all the more clearly upon the pallid features like a dull crimson stain.

It ran down the low forehead, only by a miracle escaping the right eye, trailing off just below the ear to the back of the neck. It showed all the more plainly because the pretty brown curls which Jerry had been wont to admire so much were all gone, partly burnt away, the rest sacrificed by the doctor's scissors in the height of the fever. Only a few scanty clipped locks were left, which were but insufficient to hide the cruel marks. But painful as was the change from the once pretty bright face of the little fancy-rider, such that none but loving eyes could have recognised in the weary, helpless invalid, the gay Fay of Fire, Jerry thought not so much of the loss of beauty as the evidence the change gave of the bitter struggle which had been gone through.

When Lizette saw his eyes full of pity as they were fastened upon her, she turned the scarred side of her face away from the light, as if she could not bear even him to look upon it, and said something in a low voice about having had a bad night, as if in excuse for her tired looks.

Jerry withdrew his gaze suddenly, recalling that cry of " Carl, Carl," which had kept sleep from his eyes, rest from his mind, and wondered whether it had been a repetition of it which had been wrung from the weary soul and driven away the peace of the night.

But it was nothing to do with him, if such had been the case. It was the body he had taken into his charge—the soul he left in higher hands.

He therefore made his proposition about a change of lodging.

Lizette replied she was quite contented where she was. If only he would come and see her sometimes, and if he could help her to get work, she wanted nothing else.

All those who have had anything to do with a sick person, or rather one recovering from a sickness, know what a hard battle it is to fight against complete despondency; when all desire save to be left alone, to live on as best they can —which, translated, means to die as soon as human nature has got down to the lowest ebb— seems to have fled away, leaving only a poor remnant of what had once been a being full of hope and love of life. The shadows which had crowded into the troubled mind, the growth of many days of bitter pain and loneliness, were not to be driven away at once by one breath of gladness.

The excitement of Jerry's coming having worn off in the hours of suffering in the long weary night, there was that usual sinking back into the darkness, which is ten times more difficult to overcome than the late violent despair.

Even the longing which she had before felt for some friend to come to her in her trouble, seemed, now that it was satisfied, to have been but an empty one.

The friend she longed for would not, could not, come. What, then, was the use of any amount of kindness from any one else?

No doubt this was a selfish view of the matter, but it is not at first that lessons of pain and suffering show fruit.

Besides, it must be remembered that Lizette knew nothing of the love which she was trampling so remorselessly under foot, and never knew how many a thoughtless word at her own helplessness was a wound in the brave heart which sought so hardly to bear her burden for her.

As plainly as if she spoke she said, " Leave me alone; I want no one to care for me, since he to whom I gave all I had to give loves me not. I care not what becomes of me. Leave me to myself." But Jerry was not to be so soon defeated.

Although he did not again repeat what he had said yesterday,—" Now that I have found you I will never let you go," he let his actions speak for him.

Without attempting to discuss the plans he had made, he gradually drew from the girl a clearer statement of her affairs than she had given the night before, and soon found that, as he had suspected, poverty was the one bar to any step in the right direction towards health.

" Only that?" he said, when Lizette frankly told him the little she possessed in the world. " Why, it is not enough to keep you as you should be kept for a week."

" It will have to do for many days more than

that. And I have my work. I was counting to have finished it last night, but you came, and it is yet to do."

Jerry wondered whether she regretted his coming.

" The work is not like riding," he said.

Lizette's face fell suddenly.

"This work with the needle like riding! No, no, indeed!" And a heavy sigh told the rest.

Jerry blamed himself for his want of tact, and, bringing the very short interview to a close, departed. He did not go home, however. Waylaying Sarah, who was in a high state of curiosity as to who the stranger was and what his business could be, he desired her to conduct him into the presence of her mistress. This being done, a somewhat stormy meeting ensued, in which, I believe, the young clown at length vented his pent-up feelings by favouring the landlady with a pretty big piece of his mind concerning the rate which she charged for her miserable lodgings.

Whatever policy he used, however, the result of the interview was that Sarah was, after dinner, desired to get ready a room on the third floor, which had lately been vacated by a barber's assistant—I may say forcibly vacated, since that gentleman was " wanted" by two gentlemen in uniform, who, as in the childish game of " Nuts and May," fetched him away in a cab, since which time nothing had been seen of him. Therefore Sarah, in the middle of a great cleaning of pots and pans in her regions, was bidden set to work and reduce his late apartment to order, Mrs Spicer superintending the operation, in order, it seemed, to in her turn vent her spite upon her unfortunate handmaid.

By the evening the getting-ready process was completed, and the room pronounced in order.

This fact Sarah, duly commissioned by her mistress, proceeded to announce to Lizette, who as usual at that hour was lying on her couch, thinking sad thoughts, and wondering what was the use of living if life was such a weary burden.

The sick girl, on receiving the intimation, started from her reverie, and then imagined that her friend had at last succumbed under the press of so much nagging from her mistress. Before she had time to ask for any explanation, the girl had seized a whole armful of her belongings and departed with them downstairs, her passage being accented by the loud noise made by several articles which she carried either coming in violent contact with the wall or being dropped from her arms altogether.

In a few moments she returned, slightly more black and blue about the elbows than before, and having " at one fell swoop " gained possession of the rest of the few belongings of the little fancy-rider, without so much as deigning a word in answer to any of the questions put to her, proceeded to transport them to the lower regions with the same despatch and result to her ungainly arms.

Lizette was perfectly at a loss to understand what it could all mean. The only conclusion at which she could arrive was anything but a pleas-

ant one. Could it be that Mrs Spicer for some
unknown reason had taken it into her head to
turn her out of doors? What had she done that
she should deserve it?

In fear and trembling she awaited the return
of Sarah, who, in answer to her timid question—
Sarah even looked unapproachable—burst into a
coarse laugh.

"Turn you out? No, I guess not. You're a-
coming down into the empty on the third floor."

"Coming down to the empty on the third floor?
Why, Sarah, it is a fault. I am sure it is a fault.
I have not told Mrs Spicer. I care not to go
there. It is too much. I—"

Before she could go into any further expostu-
lation, Sarah cut them short by saying shortly, " It
ain't no use for you to say nothing. Seems your
opinion ain't to be asked in the matter. I don't
know nothing about the business. All I can tell
is that in the midst of my a-tidying up downstairs " (Sarah spent most part of her time in
tidying up, but as the other part was spent in
untidying, it was hardly to be wondered at that
the effect was scarcely what one would have imagined it to have been from the indignation
which she expressed at having the operation interrupted), "in the midst of my a-doing of the
tins and things missus comes and tells me, ' The
third-floor empty is to be got ready right off,'
which being done not without as much haggling
as if we were a-getting ready for a wedding, a
spring cleaning, or a funeral, she ses to me, ' Now,

Sarah, just go upstairs and tell that young lady to be so good as to walk down.' With that she bounces off downstairs, a-going to make the parlour's tea, which, being three-and-sixpenny, she always does herself, and no bad judge of what is good, either. But there, if she likes to take her perquisites, it's her own look out. Any way, you're to come down to the room ; so you'd best be quick about it, for I don't suppose as how you'll get down them 'ere stairs alone, and I've got to go and clear up, though what time I shall get down this blessed evening is more than I can say."

At first Lizette refused to stir. She was perfectly sure there had been some mistake, but so high was Sarah's dudgeon at being unable to make her alter her decision, besides being not a little inconvenienced by being deprived of her few possessions, that at length she consented to make the required removal.

Thus when Jerry arrived an hour later, he found her safely ensconced in the " empty on the third floor," which was decidedly an improvement on the garret, which had been her former lodging. She asked of him a solution of the enigma, and received in return a short, rather confused explanation, by which she was given to understand that hitherto she had been defrauded of her rights by the redoubtable Mrs Spicer, who, under a spirited attack from the young clown, had been induced at last to act honourably.

Part of this statement at least was true, the other half, I am bound to say, was supplied by Jerry's not very brilliant imagination. Hence the confusion into which he was thrown by having to deliver it.

Mrs Spicer had, as we know, been acting anything but fairly by her poor lodger, but she was hardly one to make such a concession as would lead to so great a change in her said lodger's circumstances. Jerry had won his way partly by steady determination, partly by a far easier but rather more costly means.

But this he desired to keep a secret, so merely explained the matter by saying that he and the landlady had come to terms, which, in fact, was just what they had done.

And Lizette was such a child in the ways of the world that she made no question of the matter, of which Jerry was exceedingly glad, for, as he afterwards told himself, his faculty for lying was very defective, and if he continued in the part he had taken to himself, he would have to do all in his power to strengthen the same, or he would find himself letting out what he had decided must be kept to himself.

It so happened that Sarah, by one of those strange ways which servants have of getting ideas into their heads which no one ever intended they should have, settled in her own mind that Jerry was the sick girl's brother.

She had heard enough at odd times from Lizette to know that the oft-repeated name of Carl referred to some faithless lover, and, I suppose, deciding in her own rather ill-regulated brain that no girl who was apparently so cut up by the loss of one sweetheart could possibly have a second, she gave it out to her mistress that Jerry and Lizette were brother and sister.

The conduct of the relations somewhat tended to increase this delusion. The former, to begin with, rarely used any name but Jerry, which, as the handmaid argued, might be Jerry—anything; a most sage conclusion. Added to this, he seemed to take matters so entirely into his own hands, to go so boldly to work, to be so open and hearty in all his dealings, that any other view of his conduct seemed impossible.

Lizette, too, accepted his protection so quietly, treated his coming and going with so much indifference. Everybody knows that to a "slavey" a sweetheart means any amount of blushes, giggling, making smart, and the like.

Mrs Spicer might not perhaps have been inclined to accept Sarah's testimony had it not been that in the heat of his discussion with her, Jerry, adopting a way he had got of speaking to himself of our little heroine, referred to her as his poor little sister, meaning "in misfortune," which little slip settled the matter.

When, on the occasion of his first visit, Sarah announced Jerry's coming to Lizette by poking her head in at the doorway and saying, "Yer brother's a-coming!" if she hoped to ascertain whether the relationship was a true one or not, she saw nothing in the sick girl's manner to upset her theory.

Lizette only went on with her work slowly, never so much as raised her eyes or looked up, saying quietly,—

" He said he would come."

"Knew he was coming, and never as much as tried to smarten herself up a bit. Didn't look a bit glad to see him, and never said anything but ' Good evening, Jerry,' when he went in, as if she'd far rather he'd kept away. That's her brother, sure enough," cogitated Sarah as she retired downstairs, where at an early opportunity she imparted her opinions on the matter to her mistress.

Mrs Spicer had at first been rather suspicious, as she phrased it. Hers was a respectable lodging-house, and " she wasn't going to have any but respectable people in it," meaning, I suppose, thereby, any but people who could do as much villainy as they liked, provided they were not found out. I am afraid she would have hardly retired to rest of a night so peacefully had she overheard a certain conversation which was carried on by the supposed relations.

Jerry had not meant to say anything about what he intended to do, but he saw that if Lizette was inclined to submit quietly to his guidance, there were others who might think fit to interfere.

" Did you hear what that girl said, Liz ? " he asked, when he stood up to say good-bye on his first visit. " She thinks I'm your brother. So does the old woman. Do you mind if they go on thinking it ? "

He was afraid Lizette might even object to this title. But she shook her head. The past, the past, was all she thought of. She never saw the queer look on the honest ugly face, as Jerry held her hand for a moment, and paid no special attention to his low murmured words, " My sister ; God help me to be a brother to you."

She never knew the solemn vow which those words contained. And how was the vow kept? It remains to be seen.

CHAPTER III.

BROTHER AND SISTER.

AND so the new era in these two lives began.

There was no fuss, no arranging, not so much as a word of explanation between them. Each seemed to fall into the other's plan as readily as if it was the one of all others to be desired. It was just as well that it should have been thus, at least Jerry thought so.

He had fully made up his mind what his duty was with regard to this frail life cast thus upon his care, and meant to do it day by day, till he should reach the end he so much desired, namely, to restore the little German girl to what she was.

And Lizette let him take matters into his own hands with only a very slight show of resistance. Had she been anything but the weak, weary girl she was, she might have seen through the fence of kindness and solicitude with which little by little he surrounded her.

As it was, she looked upon him as a friend who was kind enough to interest himself on her behalf, to bring her welcome little presents now and then

when he dared—always sending them through
the medium of Sarah, who was not a little put out
when she found that the sick girl had any friend
but herself.

I do not suppose the servant girl meant her dis-
pleasure to be at all selfish, but she certainly was
jealous of the new-comer, and vented her spite by
various grimaces and gesticulations expressive of
future vengeance whenever his back was turned.

At first Lizette resolutely stuck to her old habits;
the wish to be "left alone" was her only one, and
Jerry despaired of ever arousing her from the state
of mental coma into which she seemed to have
fallen.

At first he persuaded her to give up her work
almost entirely, to let the future take care of itself.
Lizette obeyed, but he soon saw that the long
hours she spent with her hands folded on her lap
were far worse for her than when at least her
fingers were employed.

She must take to work again, he decided one
night on returning from a visit to his sick sister,
as he called her, a visit which had showed him
a sad white face, and eyes heavy with weeping.
Work would, perhaps, help her along a bit. Yes,
she must work. Oh, if only she were well enough
to go back to the old riding business, how much
more reason would he have to look forward to
seeing her herself again soon. The old business
would have been the very best medicine for her.
But there, it was no use thinking of it. She was
too weak even to crawl up and down-stairs with-

out help; of the day which should come and find
her able to take her place, it seemed hopeless to
do anything but dream.

At any rate, the sewing must answer the purpose of giving her some little aim in life; even to
reach the end of a yard or two of hemming was
better than sitting marking the flight of each
moment by a tear of weariness.

But work is not always to be found when
wanted, especially if it had been thrown aside in
a moment of heedlessness.

So Jerry found it. The mission of obtaining
such as Lizette needed was all the more a difficult
one, because he was in a city where he knew next
to no one, and was certainly not used to making
inquiries as to any one who might be in want of
the services of a seamstress.

According to the answers which he received in
reply to his rather diffident inquiries, the talent for
doing plain needlework seemed at a premium.

It so happened, however, that in trying to help
others he helped himself—namely, by discovering
in the course of one of his peregrinations that in
a distant part of the town a Hall of Varieties was
in reality a circus.

It was only a second-rate affair, but anything
was better than enforced idleness; so boldly pre-
senting himself before the authorities, he offered
his services of an evening for a very nominal sum
—about half that which he had been accustomed
to receive even from the not too liberal Charles
Petman.

But, as he told himself, anything was better than nothing, quit the town he could and would not until he saw Lizette in a measure recovered, but all the same the days hung heavily on his hands, and he looked forward with pleasure to being once more at his old tricks. There was nothing, he knew of old, kept him so much himself as steady jogging work. In the ring he forgot his troubles for the time, so in the ring he went once more, and was soon a great favourite among the numerous if hardly high-class audiences of the hall, which favour, however, did not procure for him that rise in his salary which he might justly have expected.

The management argued that if he had turned out a dead letter they would have had to suffer, meaning thereby that they would have been under the painful necessity of dismissing him, and as he had turned out the very reverse, they did not see why they should not be benefited.

The engagement, however, led to better results than even a mere monetary return. It so happened that the niece of Jerry's landlady was one day escorted by a love-lorn swain to the Hall of Varieties. The said swain was a pawnbroker's assistant of some personal beauty, but very little intellectual capacity, hence the reason of his having been captivated by Miss Jane Withers, who very kindly permitted—mind, I do not say requested—him to escort her to various places of amusement. She hoped that amidst the clamour and excitement of festivity he might in an unguarded moment be induced to give utterance to his feelings in *words*, or, to quote her own expression, " to pop."

On the occasion, however, of the visit to the Hall of Varieties, when success seemed very likely to crown her efforts, this love-lorn damsel saw her aunt's lodger for the first time in the ring.

Hitherto she had looked upon him as being beneath her notice, his apartments being rather high in the scale of floors—she never deigned to lift her eyes higher than the third floor—so to her he had been nothing more than the top-floor back —not even the dignity of front—anything but *distingué* or attractive in appearance, indeed the very last person on whom she would have thought of bestowing (unasked) her young (three and thirty years old) affections.

When, however, with his famous Houp la ! he sprang into the ring, and by way of introduction to his audience made its circle in a series of wheels, as she afterwards expressed it, he fairly took her breath away.

As we know, *vide* Mr Petman, Jerry's appearance in the war-paint, as he called his public costume, was far in advance of that of his private *tout ensemble.*

The sight of his agile figure in its many-coloured dress, his painted face with its very broad smiles, roused in the landlady's niece such a tumult of feelings that, as I have said, it fairly took her breath away. When, after various acrobatic feats—not, I am bound to say, executed

with half so much smartness as in the old days of
the Petman show, when his heart was so light it
seemed impossible to keep his heels from flying
over his head for sheer happiness—he proceeded
to exhibit his skill in conjuring, one at least of the
spectators was quite overcome with wonder.

But she was to experience a deeper sensation
yet. It so happened that in the vanishing-card
trick, Jerry, looking about for some one to assist
him in the same, some one who, to say the truth,
would not be too wide awake in watching his
movements, and having long ago decided that the
fairer sex, being flattered by the attention, usually
were the best subjects for experiment, noticed her
as the only lady in the front row of seats, a position which had been obtained for her through the
valiant efforts of the pawnbroker's assistant.

Accordingly Jerry stepped across the ring to
where she sat, and with a low bow requested her
to take a card from the pack he held, at the same
time quietly indicating one with his forefinger.

Had he as abruptly laid himself and worldly
possessions at her feet, Miss Jane Withers could
not have been more taken aback by this mild
request " to take a card." At first she blushed, at
least her ruddy cheeks assumed a deeper shade of
purple than usual, drew back with a shy little
motion of her head, which motion much resembled
a chicken with a stiff neck trying to drink, but at
length complied with the request. Imagine her
feelings when the card she " took " proved to be
none other than the Queen of Hearts !

For months afterwards did the fair Jane describe to her bosom friends the thrill — yes, the positive—nay, superlative thrill which ran over her (massive) frame on beholding the court card. So overcome was she at fate having led the object of her admiring thoughts to pay her such a pretty compliment, for be it understood she was certain it was no accident—referring to that slight indication which had guided her choice—quite forgetting the slur she cast upon the conjuror's reputation by so doing—so overcome, I say, was she at the incident, that when asked to return the card to the pack, she did so so clumsily that Jerry had to assist her. Their hands touched, and whether it was that it was part of the trick or a fact due to the lady's vivid imagination in such matters, but she declared afterwards the reward of her trouble had been a slight, very slight, squeeze of the hand.

How she did simper, to be sure, when, after a deal of shuffling, one of the grooms was requested by the conjuror to knock the pack of cards from his hand, which operation being skilfully performed, Jerry still retained one card, which he held up to the audience, the Queen of Hearts.

That trick was very successful. It completely did away with the chances of the pawnbroker's assistant. On the way home, roused perhaps by the agitation of his lady-love during the episode referred to, he at length put the long-waited-for question, namely, he "popped."

To his surprise, and, in cooler moments, his joy, his answer was a stern refusal.

"Miss Jane was sorry if he had mistaken her friendship for him for any warmer feeling. She could never be anything but his sister" (*i.e.*, which meant keeping him by a tether in case other speculations should not turn out as expected. "A bird in the hand," etc.); "of one thing she was certain, her hand should never go anywhere but where her heart was." Here the young lady blushed again, and the pawnbroker knew his fate was sealed. From that day forth the young clown had a most devoted admirer in Miss Jane. She literally haunted his path like his shadow, true, a rather substantial one. At all times when he came to or went from his lodgings, on the stairs, in the hall, in the passage, the enamoured creature waited his coming, and chained him to her side by a running fire of small talk, smiles, languishing looks, and all the other means by which she was wont to enchain her unfortunate victims.

Matters even went so far as to her taking on herself to wait upon him and otherwise look after his personal comfort. She who had hitherto declined to do more than "attend" the parlours, cheerfully ascended the numerous stairs leading to the third-floor back to carry to the hero of her romance some dainty prepared by her own fair (?) hands, a red herring, a dish of tripe with fragrant onions, the odour of which recalled forcibly to his mind the old days of Mrs Parkins' petting.

But warned as he should have been by his experience with the widow, Jerry had no suspicion of the siege which was being laid to his fortress. He thought Jane a good-natured sort of girl, given to rather queer behaviour at times, such as running full tilt into his arms in the passage, talking a great deal about his conjuring, especially the vanishing-card trick, with many mysterious allusions to the Queen of Hearts, but beyond that rarely gave her a thought. She confided in him, though why he could not tell, the story of the love of the pawnbroker's assistant, also with many mysterious allusions, which our hero, as we know, being anything but vain of his personal worth, construed into no solution to the riddle whatever. It so happened, however, that he presently discovered that she could be of use to him.

One day on his way to the hall, as usual, he paid a short visit to Lizette. Every day he tried to hope that when he saw her he would find some alteration in her for the better, one little step at least towards a better state of affairs, but always when he saw her she would be lying weak, helpless, and spiritless upon her couch, looking as white, wan, and weary as when he had first found her in her desolation. The change of apartment from the dreary attic to the far more comfortable third-floor front had hardly had as good an effect as he had hoped. The knowledge that she had some one to look after her interests had relieved her of that haunting fear of what was to become

of her in the future, but in its place was that
listless despondency which was such a dead
enemy to complete recovery. Jerry usually in
his short visits did his best to cheer her up a
bit. He went to see her twice a day, sometimes
three times if he found her particularly dull and
cheerless, but rarely stayed long; the sight of
her lying so altered and helpless always made
him long to make the days go back and see her
what she had once been, even if it brought back
to him the newness of the pain which was now
an old aching grind. He often wondered how
he could find it in his heart to laugh and joke
and tell her funny tales while the sad brown
eyes looked fixedly into the fire; but he would
have joked and laughed if his heart had been
bursting, if only he could have brought a smile
or a flush of pleasure to the pale face on the
cushions.

On the day, however, of which I write, the
brown eyes looked up into his face more than
once so wearily, that all of a sudden he lost the
thread of the funny anecdote he was telling,
cleared his throat, tried to go on again but failed,
and giving up the attempt said a hasty good-bye,
and set off to his work.

All the while he was dressing and waiting to
go on, he saw the white, tired-looking face before
him, and even when he was in the ring, Madame
Poppette—between the intervals of whose performance he took his turn, and with whom he
was no small favourite, having obligingly given

one or two extra tricks, when she had one day
felt anything but up to work, owing to a bad
attack of neuralgia, which caused her nerves to
jump far better than she did—was quite concerned; Jerry certainly was anything but "spry"
as usual. He generally managed to get himself
in working order, but to-day he had got a more
than usually severe attack of the heart-ache,
which refused to be cured even by the magic of
being in the ring, where such things as hearts are
quite out of place. Presently, however, while
walking round and round in the centre of the
ring in company with two grooms and the ring-
master, he suddenly stopped short, endued with
an idea.

Madame Poppette had laughingly declared he
must be in love to be so abstracted in manner,
and made numerous inquiries concerning who the
lady might be, when the day, and such like other
teasing queries, adding laughingly, as she took off
her cloak, preparatory to her entrance into the
ring, "Mind you tell your lady-love if she wants
any help with her trousseau. I am not above
doing plain or fancy needle-work either in the
day-time. A quarter of an hour in this costume
won't fill six hungry children, or get medicine for
a sick husband."

And away skipped the brave little woman to
flit about before the eyes of an admiring public as
gaily as if such a thing as the grub period was
unknown in her butterfly life.

Her words somehow planted themselves in

Jerry's mind, recurring with a persistency that would have put the poor heart of Miss Jane Withers all in a flutter.

Would you believe it, he actually found himself wishing that he was going to be married! and that because he would then be able to put his little sick friend in the way of getting some work.

I believe for fully three moments he entertained the idea of asking some young lady—any one, it did not matter — to marry him, solely for the purpose of causing her to want a trousseau made.

This idea, however, he very reluctantly dismissed as unpractical; for asking any one to marry him meant, as a natural consequence, his marrying her, and that was just the part of the bargain he could not make up his mind to fulfil. It would not do to run the risk of being had up for breach of promise, so this view of the matter was dismissed as likely to be too expensive.

The sudden stop which he came to in the ring was caused by a second idea which flashed across him, one indeed with which he was so enchanted that it was not until the grooms and ring-master had in course of time, as was only natural in traversing a circle, overtaken him, that he was roused to a sense of where he was.

For the rest of his "turn" he was more than usually "spry." Perhaps he wished to make Madame Poppette change her mind; but at any rate the way he leapt and twirled and threw "hand-over-handers" was hardly consistent with his imputed character of being in love.

Strangely enough, too, the very next day he had an interview with Miss Jane Withers. What passed therein would, I fear, have only served to confirm the discerning fancy-rider's opinion, could she have known.

But she did not, for the matter was only entrusted to Miss Jane under pledge of great secrecy. How the pretty, frisky Jane did blush and giggle, and languish and smile when she took the oath. From that time forth she was more like a shadow than ever in her attendance of Jerry, always full of mystery and secret communications, until I am not sure that he did not repent of the bargain he had made. He had selected Miss Jane to help him in his plan, firstly because she was about the only woman he knew in the place, besides, of course, Lizette, and secondly, because he considered that being past thirty she was enough his elder to be relied upon safely.

Poor Jane, could she only have known his true feelings, what a lot of sighs, lingering looks, and goodness knows what marks of her affection she might have spared him.

As it was, she was in happy ignorance of the misfit of the key which she believed she held to the riddle, and gushed and simpered over the commission which had been entrusted to her in a way which must surely have opened the eyes of any but such a blind, self-forgetting young person as our hero.

He thought of the scheme only as it effected the end he had in view, and never for a moment considered any side consequences.

It so happened that two or three days after his talk with Miss Withers, that lady called upon Lizette, taking with her a brown paper parcel, which she did not bring away with her.

Jerry was rather late in his visit that evening, only ran in for a moment before going to the show. He found Lizette as usual on the sofa, the parcel unopened beside her.

" Hullo ! " he said—after his usual inquiries as to how she felt, and his never despairing, " Cheer up, lass, you'll be better soon," in answer to the same reply, " Just the same, thank you," to his cheery question how she was,—" Hullo ! what's this ? "

Then he stopped and went very red, but before he could say anything, Lizette replied,—

" Some work I had brought to me to-day by a Miss Withers. She is such a strange woman. I wish I had refused it, but she would not let me."

" Miss Withers ! " repeated Jerry with a degree of innocence which, to an ordinarily awake observer would have been proof positive of his guilt ; " what sort of a woman was she ? "

He had never mentioned the beautiful Jane by any but her Christian name, and strangely enough (*i.e.*, in accordance with instructions received) Miss Withers in her interview with the little seamstress never mentioned his. Lizette, as we know, was not one to say much to strangers.

Jerry's query concerning her visitor and future employer was only in accordance with the interest he always evinced concerning everything she had to tell him.

She, however, answered the question, as she frequently did others as kind in intention, by turning away her head wearily and saying almost peevishly, "She was old, I think, and talked so much it made my head to ache. I wish she had not come."

Jerry stood for some moments after this twisting his hat in his hand, as he always did when embarrassed, then suddenly announced that he must be off.

"Good-bye, Liz," he said, taking the thin white hand in his and pressing it very gently—it looked such a tiny scrap of flesh and bone in his big brown one,—"I hope you'll feel better in the morning. Shall I come and see you to-morrow?" He always asked, and she always answered in the same weary way, "If you care to come."

"Of course I do," he replied cheerily. Then as he reached the door, "Don't get at that work unless you've a mind. I'll see this Miss Withers about it if you'd rather let it be."

With that, afraid lest after all he should commit himself, he departed. His face, as he walked through the dimly-lighted streets, in spite of his cheerful good-bye, was graver even than it had been the day before.

"If this plan don't work, I don't know what will. I thought it seemed so sure yesterday, but to-day she don't seem to take to it at all ; doesn't even care to so much as undo the parcel. It seems a sin to talk of work before her, but something must be done. I can't go on day by day seeing her like she is ; not a bit better than when I found her. How white and wan she looked, as if she hadn't so much as got a bit of strength in her. Poor child! it's been a hard blow to her." And the big brown hands clenched themselves suddenly with a return of the old feeling of bitter resentment against him who had so wantonly been the cause of such misery.

A few minutes later he was in the ring at his monkey tricks, cracking jokes and earning loud applause and laughter as the reward of his jollity.

The next day matters seemed even worse. Entering Lizette's room, he found her with the brown paper parcel open on her knees, her tears falling thick and fast on the stuffs it contained. These were materials for the lighter portion of a bride's trousseau—aprons, handkerchiefs, wool for shawls, and a good number of those pretty little antimacassars, mats, chair covers, and the like, which serve to ornament a new home.

Miss Withers had blushingly said it was part of a trousseau, and perhaps it was when she thought how it might have been her own home for which she was about to work that Lizette hid her face in her hands and let her tears fall upon the pretty things.

They were for some happy bride who was going

to marry the man she loved, while her poor little
sister was ruthlessly cast aside—some one else
preferred before her. When Jerry understood
what the tears meant, a matter which took him
some time, he very nearly betrayed himself by a
burst of contrition for his own stupidity.

He took the offending parcel in his arms and
flung it on one side, and utterly refused to let
Lizette have anything more to do with it for that
day at least, and for the rest of his visit was so
subdued and humble that I fear he did very little
towards cheering his little friend.

That night he was utterly miserable. All his
plans for Lizette's happiness and welfare seemed
to be brought to nought, and she was not a whit
the better than if he had never tried to help her
at all. He put down the failure all at his own
door, never for one instant laying any blame to
her who was so little grateful for what he tried
to do that she met him as often as not with tears,
weary, despondent looks, and sometimes even
with peevish answers to his kindly-meant inquiries.

He received them all quietly, forgiving the
fault because of the provocation, and because of
the love in his great, good, honest heart for the
poor afflicted little sister whom he had so readily
and fearlessly taken under his care till she should
be able to bear her burden by herself.

CHAPTER IV.

A GLEAM OF HOPE.

But as when the night is darkest dawn is nearest,
so, when Jerry was most despairing of ever suc-
ceeding in the mission of charity which he had
undertaken, a faint gleam of hope dawned upon
the gloom.

It was a long time even before he would admit
that it was a gleam. Its coming was very slow,
and the work of waiting, oh, so hard! But Jerry
was only too thankful to know that light *was*
coming at last, to have anything but patience.
He had made up his mind in the beginning, that
the task he had undertaken was one which meant
waiting, and he was quite prepared to do that or
anything which might lead to Lizette's happiness
in the end.

The gleam of hope to which I refer, had of
course to do with her. The work which had at
first brought such bitter memories to her heart,
proved in time to be a means of rousing her a little
from herself—the one thing of all others to be
desired.

At first, with a listless hand, she had taken the material which lay nearest at hand. The soft silk, muslin, and cotton were far easier for the thin white fingers to handle than the coarse work on which she had hitherto been engaged; but the gay-coloured ribbons and little "fal-dals" looked somewhat out of place in the hands of the pale-faced girl who lay day after day in her shabby black dress—working, now quickly and feverishly, now wearily, as if it was too much trouble to hold the needle. Often and often at first, as she sat alone, some sudden thought, some recollection of the past, would bring the ready tears to her eyes, to flow down the white cheeks and rest upon the dainty muslin and lace she held.

Jerry had at first been glad to think that the coarse sewing was supplanted by this prettier kind; but the sight of the tears always made him call himself, for the hundredth-and-something time, a fool, and the biggest blunderer that ever lived.

Jerry was very hard on himself in those days, when he was trying so manfully to fight his own battle against the love in his heart and that of his little friend, against a no less hard one—hatred of life.

But soon he had less cause to be so relentless. It was then that the gleam of hope first crept into the darkness.

He never knew when exactly it first came. He was so often disappointed. I think it really came from that first day when he had come into the dreary attic and found "little Liz," and given to her service all he had to give—life, love, heart, soul, everything—if only it could make her happy.

The first change which he noticed was that she seemed to take a slight interest in her work. She liked to see the pretty flowers and figures growing out of the grey cotton apron or antimacassar. It was work which required some taste. Her first attempts were not very grand; but, encouraged by a kindly word or two from Jerry, who never lost an opportunity to cheer and comfort her, she grew little by little to try what she could do, and so to take an interest.

She little knew how often, while her eyes were bent over the pretty flowers which were blossoming to life under her skilful fingers—the weary droop gone from the head—a pair of grey-green eyes would be watching her with an expression in them strangely at variance with the gay tale on the owner's lips.

But Jerry had learnt his lesson in those long weeks when he had been a prisoner, imagining her he loved as happy as he could. That little slip he had made when first he had realised the change in her, would never be repeated. Never, while in his ears rang that cry of bitterness from the wounded heart, "Carl, Carl, I love you so. I have no one but you."

Not till then had he fully realised how truly great was the barrier which time had placed between them. The Present he might rule as he pleased, but the Past rose up between him and the Future. He was helpless in the hands of fate.

He often wondered, when he saw the bowed head raised a little, whether at last the poor child was learning to forget. He did not as he might once have done, but never would now, that the grave of a former love might be the cradle of a future affection. No, all such dreams were passed—the memory hidden away in his heart. Henceforth, as brother to a poor weakly sister, he would win his way to a firm and lasting friendship, instead of to the love he had once hoped to gain.

It was well for Lizette that she never guessed the thoughts which filled a heart which she so often wounded. True, she never after that first day spoke of anything connected with the days when she and Carl Hermann had walked down the golden pathway of happiness together, and Jerry took his cue from her only too willingly, although he sometimes wondered whether silence was best; yet there were hundreds of little ways by which she showed how deeply the knife had struck into her heart.

Naturally, when she spoke of the Past, she could not avoid some mention of some incidents —place or day—which brought up other recollections; and often and often Jerry would pause in his flow of cheery talk, knowing by the quivering lip, the sudden movements of the head, that he was touching some sore point.

By-and-by she seemed to find a sort of melancholy pleasure in thinking and speaking of the bride and new home for which she worked.

Jerry, however, thought the subject one especially to be avoided, and always tried to put it down if he could, giving but short, not always very comprehensive answers to Lizette's wonder as to what the latter might be like—what sort of a husband she had chosen—and such like queries, usually brought to a close by a long sigh, a clasping of the little white hands over the dainty work, while the shadows of the past crept back into the childish face, making it look so strange and tired, —a gloom which it required all Jerry's merriest efforts to chase away.

One day, when Miss Withers came, on behalf of her friend, who was too busy to have a moment to spare, as she (Jane) said, to bring more work— Lizette did not get on very fast, but the pay was very liberal—the German girl so far roused herself as to make inquiries about the bride-elect.

To her surprise Jane blushed, simpered, and very nearly let out the secret—or what she imagined to be the secret,—and was only deterred from so doing by the remembrance of the conditions under which it had been imparted to her.

Lizette thought her manner rather strange, especially for one so advanced in years. When Jerry came to pay his usual visit in the evening, she gave him a description of her employer's manner, that he too very nearly betrayed his knowledge of the original.

"Why should she blush?" Lizette said, stitching

away quickly at a pretty bunch of pink roses on a
dark velvet ground, the most extravagant piece of
work she had yet attempted. "Why, upon my
word—my word—is it? I was about to think she
is the bride herself."

Jerry burst into a hearty laugh, such had not
echoed in the room for many a long day ; then
thinking Lizette looked inquiringly at him, broke
off suddenly with a lame excuse, that from the
little seamstress's description, the lady seemed
anything but likely to be a bride, then or at any
other time, "But," he added, perhaps feeling a
twinge of conscience at not defending the friend
who was serving him, "I dare say she's a good-
natured sort of girl enough when you know her."

"Good-natured," repeated Lizette. "Yes, but
who could think of her face resting on such a
cushion as I mean to make this to be. She's
not a bride as I like to think will have any
work."

Jerry decided in his own mind that the work
of the little white fingers would be thrown away
on such an unromantic (how little he knew !) person as Jane Withers.

"Is't for her?" he said, laughing again ; then
again stopping short, and adding hastily, "They
might as well be for me, when I get married."

"For you when you get married," repeated
Lizette reflectively, adding with a sigh, "yes, I
suppose you will get married some day. I hope
she will be somebody nice, Jerry."

The words stung Jerry's brown cheeks into a

hot flush, and he was glad to be able to bend down and mend the fire.

"Married," he said, after a moment, feeling he must say something to break the silence, and of course saying the very thing he might have left unsaid. "Marry! I shall not marry till you do."

"Till I do," said Lizette, slowly untying a knot in her thread. "You must not wait for me. I shall not be married now."

Jerry hearing again the cry of "Carl, Carl," hastened to change the subject, while he laid another clod on the grave of his love.

"Those are pretty roses," he said. "But why are you making them pink. Did you not say only yesterday that they were to be white."

"Yes, but I do not like white roses."

Jerry recalled to mind the day when his modest little bunch of violets had been allowed to fade in the sawdust, while a bunch of white roses had been carefully guarded. That day was the one on which he first began to understand that he was "too late."

But in spite of these little slips now and then, matters certainly were on the mend. Lizette, it was true, was very little better in health, in spite of the good and nourishing food which Jerry insisted should be bought with the money earned by her work. She rarely now thought of the day when it should rain. I suppose because every day was alike gloomy to her, but improved in spirits she certainly was.

She must have been very low down indeed had

she been impervious to all the young clown's efforts to cheer her up. Never a visit did he pay her, but he seemed determined to make her look at the bright side of everything, always full of a fair amount of gaiety, never too loud or boisterous, but always as kind and gentle as a woman. As Lizette seemed to rally a bit, he grew even more unresting in his determination to draw her out from among the shadows, until it seemed he must triumph in the end.

Matters went on in this way for some weeks, he coming and going as freely as a brother, she being guided by him in all things as if she were truly his sister, not a word passing between them but such as was warranted by the relationship.

Jerry was honest and true to the bottom of his heart, and Lizette was after all but a child in the ways of the world, and knew no fear.

So, as Jerry had hoped, hand-in-hand, as it were, they went through life together, he wanting no greater, more grateful task than to be her guide and protector. When he saw her gradually losing the old despairing self, he rejoiced as only a brave unselfish heart could, and prayed the change for the better might go on.

And it did go on, till at length the day came when he persuaded the long caged bird to try her wings in the fresh spring air.

But she shrank from quitting her prison. There are some prisoners to whom the cell becomes in time a home which they are loath to leave.

Jerry did not press the point. He never commanded—only suggested quietly and gave way to any objection — usually, however, ending by having his own way.

In this case, however, all his efforts proved unavailing, and when he saw the thin hands clasp themselves with the old gesture of pain over the scarred face, he could not find it in his heart to say more.

But when the days grew warmer he would fling the window wide open, and let the soft air and the golden sunshine stream into the dingy room. At first Lizette seemed even afraid of the yellow beams seeing her so different to what she had once been; but after a little she grew to love the change from the gloom and chill of the winter to the mild bright days of spring.

She did not know it, but the winter in her heart was slowly giving place to the softer season, and even Jerry did not fully comprehend the change.

He did not know how at last the sunshine was breaking through the clouds and dispelling the gloom.

And then, when all seemed going on so smoothly —when peace and content were gradually coming into the troubled hearts—a shadow suddenly fell across their path and turned the sunshine into darkness.

It so happened that one day, entering his dressing-room at the Hall of Varieties, Jerry found himself face to face with an old friend, or rather, I should say, an old acquaintance—none other than George Epsom.

The jockey returned his greeting in his usual surly manner, and did not express any joy at the meeting. Jerry had never let him make any unpleasantness between them, but Epsom was down in his luck a little, and did not choose to be civil to any one. When the young clown began to question him concerning the Petman Show and the phenomenon of the vans having been seen by him in the brewer's yard, he told him shortly to go and ask Madame Petite what he wanted to know, —her tongue was long enough to answer any amount of questions.

By-and-by, however, in the course of dressing, he vouchsafed a strongly-worded account of what had occurred to the show after it left the People's Gardens, part of which history, up to the time of Lizette's accident, Jerry was already acquainted with.

To his no small regret and surprise the young clown learnt that the Petman Show was "no more,"—it was dead, or, to be more explicit, broken up. Not many days after he had so cruelly left the girl whom he and his daughter had treated so unjustly, and who had been so faithful in her services to him, to struggle back to life or to die amidst strangers, while once again exerting his powers of wrath upon an unoffending wretch, Mr Petman fell down in the fit which had long seemed inevitable.

Very little hopes were entertained of his recovery; at any rate he would never more be any use at his old work. His daughter and her husband, who, it is to be hoped, took the opportunity of showing forth in better colours than hitherto, took care of the father thus striken down as it seemed by the hand of justice in the midst of his vile wrath; the company of the show was dismissed to get engagements elsewhere as fortune might be favourable or no, and the vans and other properties were stowed away until a purchaser could be found for them.

Jerry was not one to bear resentment long, though he did not pretend to be a paragon. The insult which Lizette had received from the hands of Mr Petman he never would forgive, but when he heard of the old man's fate he could think of him pityingly at least, and say, "Poor old chap, it's a fearful punishment," believing that when a debt is paid in this life for some sin, it is not again charged to the offender in the next.

But if he could pity Mr Petman for what was past, he had much ado to keep down his own angry feelings when the jockey, referring to Lizette's accident, spoke in terms anything but gentle.

"The girl was a fool; they all are. Old Petman was—well, right when he told her so. Hadn't more pluck than a baby. Always moping about with a die-away look in her face, as if there wasn't another man in the world. Bah! it makes me sick. Hermann was a—conceited young puppy, but—" And then followed opinions and views of the whole matter, which so roused Jerry that while he was debating in his own mind how to convey to the jockey's mind the fact of his adopted relationship to the object of his scorn and contempt, he (Epsom) hurried out of the tent to see that Daredevil was in proper trim, as it was important he should give a successful performance on that, the first, evening.

Left alone, Jerry vented his rage by nearly strangling himself with his necktie, in his efforts to remove it while tied, by a series of wrenches, after which display of feeling he grew calmer.

And growing calmer, he began to quietly consider the matter—namely, his unexpected meeting with the jockey, and what it might lead to. Into his thoughts we will not pry. Certain it is they are honest and pure. I think we know Jerry a little by this time.

At any rate, he determined upon some course of action, for when a little later he met Madame Petite in the ante-room, he had no time save for a hurried greeting, so gave her no time to justify the jockey's remark concerning her talking powers. She would no doubt have liked to have had a chat with him over affairs of the now dispersed show, but neither then nor the following days did Jerry seem to have a moment to spare if she came near.

He mentioned to Lizette the fact of her old friend being in the town. The invalid said she should like to see her old friend, and expected her for some days, but as she did not come, never thinking that Jerry had not told of her whereabouts, she put it down as the jockey's fault, and said no more.

For about a week Jerry managed to avoid the little woman, but at the end of that time, on going to pay his usual visit at Mrs Spicer's, he learnt that Madame Petite had bethought herself of inquiring at her friend's old address, on a chance of finding her still there, and, of course, been successful.

She had been greatly grieved at the change in the little Fay of Fire,—had fairly broken down— and, hugging the shorn lamb to her motherly breast, had cried over her, unable to say a word save,—" *Pauvre petite, pauvre cherette. Ah mais comme il est terrible, comme il est terrible, pauvre petite.*"

Her visit hardly did as much good as might have been expected from the tone of her sympathy.

When Jerry arrived, he found Lizette hardly so cheerful as usual, and heartily wished the un-offending Frenchwoman at the bottom of the sea.

Like a sensible being, however, he did not notice the depression in the air, but set to work to clear it, till, little by little, the sick girl grew more lively.

He did not ask her what had passed between her and Madame, although he would very much have liked to have known. He supposed Lizette had told the whole story. There was nothing to do but to hope her listener would see matters in the right light, and hold her tongue.

It seemed that she did and could do this, in spite of the jockey's assertion; and surely no one who had heard the sick girl's tale could think of evil against her and her protector.

At first when she knew but half the truth, Madame Petite's face had fallen suddenly, and a strange, almost frightened, look had crept into her eyes as they rested on Lizette. Perhaps she was thinking of the days when, in innocence and helplessness, far, far less than that of this little German, she had been led away by one who had seemed to be her friend.

She could make no effort to break her own chains, but there was enough good in her withered old heart to shrink from the thought of seeing others wilfully forge theirs.

She remained for a few moments without speaking, then asked softly, so loath was she to breathe the first breath of evil,—

" And so Monsieur Jerri has been your guardian angel, as they say ? "

Lizette nodded.

" Yes, he has been very good to me. I do not know what I should have done without him. He has been my brother."

The words were simply spoken, and the brown eyes were raised so frankly to the old woman's face, that she could not but believe them ; but I think she deemed it best to keep the story to herself.

On the evening of her visit, when Jerry said good-bye, Lizette looked up suddenly from where she sat, her hands busy with a soft white woollen shawl.

" What name do you think Madame Petite gave you when I told her how good you have been for —to me ? "

It was the first time she had so openly expressed any sense of his friendship, independently of her usual thanks. Jerry paused in buttoning up his coat, then asked gaily,—

"Some ''ette,' I suppose, or some crack-jaw expression."

"No, she said it in English. She said 'Monsieur Jerri.'" Jerry began laughing; his funny name Frenchified sounded very strange. "Monsieur Jerri is a guardian angel."

Jerry flung his hat into the air, and laughed even more loudly.

"A guardian angel! The poor old lady's eyesight must be defective. I am sure I do not look a bit like one—do I now?"

Lizette looked him up and down, then shook her head.

"No; I do not think it."

Although he was perfectly aware that the reply was just—far from having even the most remote resemblance to an angel of any sort, he was, as we know, the most ordinary-looking of young men possible to behold—especially in his present costume of smoky grey and boiled yellow, the usually bright tie, and his countenance by no means altered in any one feature since we first saw it—yet I think Jerry was a trifle disappointed at the decided denial.

Perhaps he showed as much in his face, for Lizette looked up with one of her rare smiles.

"You do not look like an angel; but I think you are a—a—oh, I do not know what you call it."

" Call what ? " asked Jerry, trying hard not to be too interested.

" Some one who is good and kind, and takes care of poor girls when there is trouble, and never seems to mind how cross and tired they are."

"Oh, that's all nonsense," broke in the would-be angel with great earnestness. " I only did what anyone ought to have done—that is," not liking to cast a slur upon other people's charity, " only that I liked to do." Then thinking this expression might mean more than he intended, or rather more than he wished it to, he added, " I'm your brother, you know. If I can't help you along a bit, I don't know who can."

" But, all the same," said Lizette, " what did you call Signor Patchouli when he let me ride the Turk ? "

" A brick, or something like that," said Mr Angel, forgetting to what end the questions were leading.

" Then you are a brick," said Lizette, with a quiet emphasis which contrasted curiously with the slang her companion had put into her mouth.

Jerry laughed more heartily than before, whereupon, with something of a return of her old manner, Lizette shook her head at him, saying he was very rude, and for once did not suddenly return to her old depressed mood.

When Jerry said good-bye, he asked as usual if he might come again on the morrow, and received the usual answer, " If you care to ; " but this time Lizette added, " Why do you ask always? You know you may come. I can't get on—without—my guardian angel—I mean, my brick."

And Jerry went home feeling more light-hearted than he had done for many days.

He contrived sometimes to pay his visit when Madame was expected—meeting the old woman's glance so frankly and honestly that she did not dare say the word of warning she meant to have uttered.

Once, when they left the house together, she did say,—

"Monsieur Jerri, you mean always to take as good care of the child as you do now?" and she fixed her keen little grey eyes on his face.

"Yes, Madame," he said quietly, returning the look. "She is my sister."

"You are a good man," replied the little French-woman, clasping his arm tightly. "It would be a different world if that there were more like you. But it is dangerous."

Jerry made no reply, and the matter dropped.

CHAPTER V.

WHAT THE BREEZE DID.

So the days went by; and as the summer came the change in Lizette grew more and more marked. Whether it was that Madame's influence, and that of Whisky, the blind kitten, was at work, I cannot say, but certain it was that the little invalid seemed less fragile in appearance than she had been, while she grew to take more pains in keeping her room bright and cheerful.

Knowing how fond she was of flowers, Jerry had often brought her such as he could procure; but she seemed at first to have lost even her taste for this. The winter's blossoms were often left to die and wither for want of fresh water. Now they were placed carefully in the window where the sun could get at them, carefully tended, or sometimes on the table at which the little seamstress worked, where, as they did not thrive so much, the table was moved to the window, an arrangement which answered two purposes—the flowers got the air and sunshine, and so did the human and no less fragile blossom, the two combined making the best medicine possible for the wasted frame.

The view of the street which, too, she got from the window gave Lizette a little amusement while she sat at work. She grew to know by sight the more regular passers-by, and to wonder where they came from and what their business was ; but it was some time before she could bear to meet any glance which they might cast up at her, even though she always sat with the poor scarred side of her face turned away.

She could not even now sit upright for any great length of time—the injury to her back was anything but slight, but Jerry managed, by means of some old properties, as he called them—the same including a big thick shawl, which was anything but old—to make an old arm-chair into a fairly comfortable reclining chair for her to use when she felt inclined. Neither of them guessed what a source of interest they were to one of the occupants of the houses opposite—an old artist— who saw Jerry come and go regularly, now whistling gaily, now seemingly cast down, usually with some little gift—a few flowers, or some dainty such as might tempt a poor appetite.

First of all, a dim shadow now and then on the blind in the third floor front was all this unknown observer could make out of the sister, then he saw behind the curtain some one sitting at work, then the flowers would be put out on the window sill, giving the watcher a glimpse of a white face, which by-and-by was more clearly seen as the days grew warmer, and the little seamstress sat for some time at the open window.

At first she did so for a little while, now and then rising and going away quickly if any one seemed to look up curiously at her, but after a little she generally was to be seen at certain times, those times when the very devoted brother would come flinging along down the street to pay his usual visit.

Perhaps at first she did it because she knew he wished it, but soon it was observed that she seemed to take particular interest in that end of the road from whence he came, although returning his nod of recognition with very little warmth— at least it was so at first; by-and-by the brown head with its short curls would lean forward as if to make sure it was he; then a wave of the hand would be given, ere long, accompanied by a smile of welcome, which altered the sad face wonderfully.

The flowers, too, which he brought were sometimes now fastened in the little black dress, taking away its sombre appearance; and sometimes, when he was seen in the distance, the thin white hands would smooth down the ruffled hair, and make such little signs of preparation as laying aside some coarse work (Lizette had found other customers by this time, but still did a little work for Miss Withers' friend) for some dainty little "faldal" which he would often take up in his big fingers and handle with the greatest care and

reverence, such as would bring a smile to her face
—her smile always in response meeting his hearty
laughter. All this and a good many other little
scraps of evidence of the change which was going
on so slowly but surely in the room on the third
floor was seen by the old artist as he sat day by
day at his work in the window opposite. He often
used to lay down his brush and think how nice it
was to see a brother and sister so fond of each
other; but then you see the old man was a little
soft in the head, so it was not to be expected he
would attach any particular importance to signs
which would very soon have been rightly construed by a farther-seeing person.

He grew in his queer sort of way to be very
fond of the white face opposite; indeed, after
regarding it across the street for many many days,
it found its way on to his canvas. He began
many pictures, but rarely finished one. How he
lived was a mystery; but it was believed he had
a very rich sister who allowed him just enough to
live upon, provided he did not trouble her any
further. No wonder he thought in his simple way
that all brothers and sisters are not all alike.

The picture he began to paint of his all-uncon-
scious little model across the way, he called by
some strange fancy "The Angel Sister." It was
just a frail girlish form, with a sweet face, smiling
down as if in welcome from a mass of floating
fleecy clouds—at least such it was at first. He
altered it afterwards; the smile gave place to a
look of helpless fear; the eyes, which before had

been so soft and tender, had a look in them of a hunted animal; the white robe was changed to one of dull grey, and the fleecy clouds became storm messengers black and dense above the drooping head. He called this picture "Lost." When, not long after the white face of the little sister had vanished for ever from the window opposite, news was brought to the rich cold-hearted lady that her brother was dead, and she sent some one to dispose of his few belongings, there were some who said that had the old man lived, that picture "Lost" would have made his name and fortune.

But it was too late to talk of earthly reward then. So the one finished work was hidden away in some obscure corner, as the painter had been, and never won the fame which was really due to it.

But Lizette knew nothing of the model she was serving, she saw the old artist sometimes when she sat at her window, but never guessed the close watch he kept upon her,—never guessed that she had any motive for the actions he saw,—never knew ; but there, let me tell all things in order.

It so happened that her birthday came round. Remembering how she had spent the last one, she determined to let it slip by unnoticed. But Madame Petite—wilfully, I believe—let out the secret to Jerry, and he at once entered into a conspiracy to make it a high day and holiday— the first Lizette had known for many a long day. So when the little seamstress woke on the day she was to forget, it was to find

Sarah blundering into the room with two letters containing two birthday cards, most gorgeous in design, and profuse in good wishes, and two parcels, one containing a big white shawl such as she had lately worked with so much care for Miss Withers' friend, whose wedding, by-the bye, was a long time coming, the other sundry little "faldals," as Jerry called them—a pretty lace collar, an apron with rosy bows, and one or two other cunning little wherewithals to lighten a sombre toilette.

The gifts were not much in themselves, but the kindly thought—more kind even than she guessed —was grateful to the recipient.

A little later Madame herself arrived, bringing with her the news that at half-past two a carriage would be at her Majesty's door to take her for a drive.

I am sorry to say Lizette received the announcement with anything but pleasure—indeed, at first she persisted she would not stir out of the house. But the little Frenchwoman did battle with her objections in right royal manner.

"Not come out!" she said, affecting the greatest surprise, though she knew well enough what she had got to expect. "Not come, when Monsieur Jerri has taken the trouble to get an easy carriage for you,—gone all the way to the stables at the other end of the town to be sure the horse is good—for he said, 'It would not do for it to bolt with our invalid; he must go gently—very gently—for it is her first little excursion, and we must be careful.' So he has gone to get a quiet horse and a nice carriage. And see what a lovely day it is—Jerri calls it Queen's weather. Oh! you must come. He has made it a surprise for you. He will be so disappointed."

But the poor little bird still shrank from quitting the cage in which she had been a prisoner so long. She quietly but resolutely resisted all Madame's arguments, and steadily refused to consent to the plan.

The old woman did her best, but when the morning passed, and all her efforts proved unavailing, she lost her temper, and could fairly have shaken her little friend.

"You are an obstinate child—a perfect baby," she said wrathfully. "You do not deserve that Monsieur Jerri should be so kind. He will be so disappointed. You know he will. He would do anything in all the world for you. And you—you are so stupid—so ungrateful. You care no more for him than for my little finger."

"Care for him," repeated Lizette, going on quietly with her work. "I care for him like my brother."

"Brother—bah! I thought you had more sense. Can't you see how he—" Madame stopped short, for Lizette's big eyes were fixed wonderingly on her, the look of innocence in them perfectly unmistakable.

"Can I not to see what?" she asked, getting, as usual when excited, perplexed in her English. "What have I not eyes for?"

"For what is good for you," replied Madame shortly, letting the reply stand in what light it might.

A silence followed. Lizette went on with her work, and Madame vented her indignation by sewing away at some coarse stitching as if her life depended on it. She never even deigned to glance at her companion. Had she done so, she would have seen on her face a puzzled look, as if she was at a loss how to solve some riddle.

Presently she seemed to give up the attempt, and began talking lightly of other things—doing, meanwhile, far from good with her needle.

To this fact Madame ironically called her attention.

" I am afraid I shall have to take your advice and be lazy on my holiday," Lizette said, and soon the work was entirely laid aside.

Then she walked with the slow step which was all she had strength for now, very unlike the gliding tripping of formerly, up and down the room, picking up scraps and pieces, moving the furniture, and giving the little vase of roses on the table fresh water for the second time that morning—though flowers were far more plentiful then than they were when she had cared so little for them—in fact behaving as if she thought the room looked hardly festive enough for the occasion.

Having brought about some very slight change for the better in her room, she effected a transformation in herself. The dingy, shabby black dress was replaced by a sober but far prettier grey one, made simply, but sadly showing the alteration in the wearer's thin figure from the rounded one it had once been. At the neck she fastened the collar—Madame's present, donned also the apron with the rosy ribbons, and ran her fingers through the still rather short curls. This done, she sat down in the low chair at the window, where the keen grey eyes of the little French-woman watched her all the while they seemed intent on the coarse work, and the other pair of watery blue ones across the street did the same.

"Ah," said the old artist when he saw the change of costume, "zee leetle schild"—he was a German also—"zee leetle schild is to be happy herselves to-day. She haf some joy. She haf put away zee ugly dress and haf a pretty one. And now she is come for to vatch for her brusser. Zare—she sit still for some moments — she is thinking—zen she begin to look for him, although it is not yet zee time. Ah, and now she haf put some of his flowers in her bosom, and looks down at zeem as if to say, He will like me to wear zeem. He is a good brusser, and she has right to look for him. Hah, if I had a sistare—a sistare like to her. She is so pretty and so good. He is not pretty, but I think he must be good, and— Here he come. Look out, little sistare, here he come. Ah, she haf see him, she haf lean forward to wave her hand and smile. How pretty she look when she smile. He is pleased. He wave his hat, and very near knock over zat leetle boy. Zare, it is just like to him— give him a penny and pat his head. She laugh. She know he is clumsy, but she—"

At that moment the landlady enters with her lodger's so-called dinner, and the old artist's soliloquy is cut short before he can give a name to his "angel sister's" feelings towards her brother.

Meanwhile, arguing well from his little friend's unusually gay greeting, Jerry hardly waited to say good-day to Sarah, who opened the door, and with whom he was by this time no small a favourite, but went bounding upstairs two steps at a time.

His hopes, however, received a blow when, on entering the third-floor front, Madame Petite informed him with great precipitation that he had better set off at once and countermand his order of the carriage, as Lizette resolutely refused to set foot outside the house.

Jerry's hopes fell suddenly, but he said nothing, only crossed to where Lizette stood, the smile of greeting still on her lips, and shook hands with her, at the same time laying on the table a beautiful bunch of roses which he carried.

"Not going! I am sorry for that, Liz. I hoped you would like it—but never mind."

I think if he had looked the least bit put out or annoyed, or even crestfallen, as he sometimes did when his plans failed, Lizette would have liked it better.

She did not offer to take the flowers, but turned away to the window, putting up her hands to her face with the old gesture, which told the reason for her refusal.

There was silence. Madame had a reason for saying nothing, contenting herself with looking the more, and Jerry, as usual, could think of nothing to say on the spur of the moment.

Presently Lizette turned away from the window and said slowly, " I will go, Jerry, please."

Jerry did not at all like the look of this humble surrender. He was afraid Lizette might think he wanted to tyrannise over her—the very last idea in his mind. In his bungling way he tried to make her understand that she had only herself to please in the matter, ending by giving her to understand that he did not in the least care whether she went or stayed at home, a statement which, when she persisted in her determination to do the former, his manner entirely contradicted.

A little later a comfortable basket carriage, drawn by a very sober-looking grey pony, drew up at Mrs Spicer's door, from whence in a few minutes the artist at the window saw issue forth the little white-faced girl in the grey dress, lightly wrapped up in a big woollen shawl—the day was so warm—her face half hidden under a big straw bonnet, her hand shielding the scarred side of her face (Lizette had wanted to wear a veil, but Madame had scouted the idea, and Jerry looked rather grave, so it had been given up). She was leaning on the arm of her brother, who looked particularly

jovial and happy. He assisted her carefully into
the carriage, placed a rug over her knees, insisted
upon her having an extra cushion for her back, at
her wish unfurled a big umbrella to keep off the sun.

The little old woman took the seat back to the
horse, and, taking the reins from the boy, the
brother sprang into the seat beside his sister, and
the pony started. The next moment they had
disappeared down the sunny street. That afternoon, the old artist did even less work than usual.
He was on the watch for the return of the pleasure
party. But the afternoon went by, and he watched
in vain. It was not until dusk that they returned.
There was, however, just light enough to see the
flush of health and enjoyment which glowed in
the invalid's usually pale face. On her lap she
held a big bunch of flowers. Jerry assisted her
into the house—saw her comfortably seated in
her chair at the window, then he and Madame
set off at the top of their speed for the Hall of
Varieties. The old artist was at his window all
the evening, looking across to where the face of
the angel sister showed in the room opposite. She
must have been very tired with her excursion, for
after bending forward to wave a regretful good-
bye to her companions, she lay back in her chair
and hardly moved, sitting looking out into the
dim light as if lost in thought.

Fully two hours went by thus, and still she did
not move. The old man over the way watched
her curiously, though now the dim outline of her
face was all he could see.

Presently as it grew later, among the crowd in the street came a young fellow, who walked quickly till he came within sight of the window in Mrs Spicer's third-floor front, then slackened his speed. When he saw the face at the window he went a little faster—passed the house—paused, and whispered softly to himself with a sigh, "Good-night, little sister, God be thanked I may do even this much for you—I ask no more."

And when he turns on his way, a deep sigh rises to his lips. Ah, how different is what is, to what might have been.

Up in that darkened room above the girl still sits motionless. She, too, is thinking of Past, Present, and Future, but the first seems lately to have become farther off—the veil which hangs over it thicker—the darkness which divides it from the light more and more dense, hiding from sight the unfaith and unrest which lie beyond. Slowly, as she has done very often of late, Lizette is going over the scenes of her later life.

Once she could not even trust herself to do this—the glare of the treacherous gaslight made all else seem so gloomy. Then slowly, she hardly knew how, in her heart she said, "The light is not for me—it would be a sin," meaning she must bury her love, now that her lover was another woman's husband. At first this had seemed impossible, but pride had made the grave, and time slowly filled it in, almost without her knowing it.

And as day after day laid a clod upon the

mound, slowly but surely from the once darkened sky a ray of golden sunshine—the sunshine of a pure and unselfish love—fell upon the drooping flower, and insensibly warmed and gladdened it into life.

Only very very slowly had the work been done, —so slowly, progress there seemed none—but then when people wilfully blind their eyes, how can they be expected to see plainly?

As she sat in the window on that warm spring evening, the sick girl's mind more than half unconsciously reviewed the days which seemed so long ago, and with the days came faces which she knew—one in particular, the day when first on that wet evening she had made her way to the Petman Show, one face more willingly than the rest. The day when she had first made her appearance in the ring among the Petman people; again recalling a face,—the days which followed —that memorable walk into the country. Ah, yes! that day "he" who was dead to her now had laid the first stone in the edifice which was one day to fall about her ears with a mocking sound. The poor child sighed as she recalled it, but smiled the next moment when she recalled the funny little incidents of the walk — her companion's queer behaviour — the strange way his manner kept altering from grave to gay and back again—the episode of Joe the old carter, and a heap of things which happened at the same time. Then the days when her friend, as she called him, was away. She skipped

hurriedly over these, for they belonged to the
buried joy. The day when the white roses and
the violets had been given to her. The roses
were still in the little satin box—untouched lately,
—the violets—where were they? It must have
looked very ungrateful to have taken so little
care of them; but never mind, the other flowers
which the same kind hand had brought since
then were carefully guarded—some at her bosom
even now. The day when she had so nearly
been hurt by Miss Petman's inability to reduce
Daystar to order,—the soft words which had been
whispered in her ear—false, false, every one of
them,—the irksome imprisonment which some one
had had to suffer for her sake. The funny tea-
party at Mrs Parkins', and some parts of the conversation, which it seemed perfectly useless to
remember. The grand day at the Gardens, every
incident of which was recalled, from the first
donning of the pretty dress to the riding home
in the omnibus,—the babies—the mastering of one
of them,—the man in the stiff collar and black
gloves,—the thin young man with the parcel,—the
lady in the bonnet,—the comments upon her companion's good nature — comments which Lizette
hardly remembered to have heard, but which all
came back again. Then the dreary days before
and after the accident, all coming to an end in
that day when her friend had come and found her
so lonely and so sad, and had kissed her—yes,
she wondered why she had not remembered that
before. He had kissed her and said something

in a queer voice, which she was too faint to
hear. Then more days, seeming all alike as they
had gone, but each now that they were recalled
bearing some slight record of never-ceasing kindness and goodness. Then, last day of all—the
one drawing even now to its close—the one in
which she recalled faces from the past—two, oh,
so very different to look upon, and one gradually
making the other vanish into the gloom which
time had hung over what was.

And which face is it that so slowly has grown
out of the darkness? I do not think even the
dreamer would give it a name if you asked her.

She sits looking dreaming out into the dimly-
lighted street, a far-away look in her eyes. She
sees among those who pass and repass a figure—
a very ordinary one. A gleam from a lamp falls
on the face. Though it is not looking up at her,
she smiles and waves her hand as if dreaming
still. She watches the figure out of sight, still
with the same strange look on her face. When
it turns the corner of the street and disappears
from view, she leans forward as though to call
it back.

The action seems to rouse her to herself. She
starts like one awakening from sleep, looks quickly
round her as if afraid of being watched; then,
pushing her hair off her face, rises, crosses the
room, and takes from a drawer a little satin-
covered box. This she carries to the window,
takes a little key from a chain which she wears
round her neck, and unlocks it. A few withered

flowers, dry and brown, the remains of what were once so fresh and fair, are all it contains.

She turns them over with her thin fingers, but no tears fall upon them now as they have done so often before. Presently she rests her scarred cheek on her hand, as if they remind her of the change in herself; and after a little is dreaming again.

We will not intrude upon her thoughts this time. The ashes of a dead love are sacred.

And yet the light in the brown eyes as they look into vacancy seems to tell of more than smouldering embers.

So she dreams on, with the evening breeze softly kissing the flushed cheeks, and nestling among the short brown curls. But it does more than this. It plays with the roses fastened above the fluttering heart, caresses them gently, plays with them, and whispers its mission to them. By-and-by it grows more bold—twines round their slender stems, bids them loosen their hold, and softly, silently, they fall upon their withered sisters.

But the breeze has not done its work yet. It does not seem to like the mournful contrast of living and dead. So it plays with the dead roses now, till presently, as they grow fearless, it rushes unawares on them and carries them greedily away—away—away into the darkness and gloom—into the noise of the street—to fall into the dirt and be trampled under foot.

Thus, when the dreamer awakes once more

the treasure-box is empty save for the fresh, fair flowers—as if the past had flown away with its burden of sorrow and pain, and left only the blooming present.

So while Jerry goes on his way saying to himself " Good-night, my sister "—as the angel sister closes her eyes upon her happy day—she presses her lips to the beautiful roses, and she too says good-night to—somebody.

CHAPTER VI.

THE ANGEL SISTER.

BUT during the night one of the fresh roses, a beautiful bud, fell from the vase, and began to fade. It was only by dint of great care that it was at length brought to bloom like the rest.

This meant that not all at once would the flowers of a new life spring forth and blossom; that a storm cloud was once more gathering in the sky; that the old artist would complete his angel sister picture, and call it " Lost."

For the story reached even his ears, and he no longer watched with pleasure the brother and sister over the way, but shook his head mournfully, and said in his childish way, " It is sad, very sad for one so young, to be so vicked. Her face, it was like to zat of an angel, but it is not. All zee woman are like to it, but it is sad in one so young."

And so he altered his picture, and gave it its new name.

The morning after her birthday, Lizette woke with that enjoyable feeling that something pleasant had happened. She lay for a little, recalling

the events of the previous day, and the sensation
rather increased than otherwise. Presently she
began to get up ; but when she went to take down
the old black dress from its peg, she paused, turned
over and over its shabby folds, and at length hung
it up again—donning instead the pretty grey one
which she had worn in honour of yesterday. She
put on the lace collar ; but thinking, I suppose,
that that was too great extravagance, laid it aside
—substituting instead a neat linen one. This
arranged, she did what she had not done for many
days—gave herself a good inspection in the glass,
not content with the view it gave on the wall, but
carrying it to the window, so that the sunlight fell
full upon the face it reflected.

At first she sighed to see how little it was still
like what it had once been, but was vain enough to
smile when she saw the brown curls were gradually becoming thick on the shorn head. All the
morning she sat at work, full in the glare of the
sunshine : I verily believe because she thought a
little colour would improve her pale cheeks.

At any rate, the golden light seemed to have an
effect upon her spirits ; for after laying down her
work more than once to lean forward a little out
of the window—I suppose to look at some object
of interest in the street below—she suddenly began
plying her needle very quickly, and all at once
commenced to sing one of those pretty German
songs which she used to sing in days long ago.
She was still singing when Jerry, a moment or
two later, came bounding up the stairs, as usual,

three steps at a time. Hearing the song, he stayed still in wonder to listen, but it broke off suddenly.

Truth to tell, the singer had heard his coming, and aware of the meaning of the words she sang—forgetting he would not understand them—she brought the song to an abrupt conclusion.

But he did not know this. He thought that some chord in the singer's memory had been touched by the sound of the mother tongue—the tongue in which her love tale had been told; and he sighed softly, and said, " Poor child."

The " poor child's " manner when she greeted him did not tend to dispel the illusion. She made no attempt to rise from her chair—only looked up and said quietly, " Ah, Jerry! is that you ? "

Just as if she expected some one else. The next moment, when he made his usual kind inquiries as to how she felt, she suddenly interrupted him, by asking very gravely, almost severely, " What for have you come ? "

" What for have I come ? " repeated Jerry, looking across at her in astonishment. " Why have I come ?—why—to see you, of course."

" I am sure I am much obliged, sir," was the mocking reply.

" Obliged to me for coming to see you ! Why, Liz, child, what ails you ? "

The expression of bewilderment on Jerry's face as he put the question, plainly showed that he thought his little sister's brain must have turned during the night.

Lizette smiled a singularly bright smile, and letting fall her work she said quickly,—

" I wonder you haf come again."

" Why the dickens shouldn't I ? "

" Why ? Because that I was so—what is the word ?—ungrateful yesterday."

" Ungrateful ! How—what ? "

" Don't bricks like to be thanked when they are good and kind ? "

" But there was nothing to be grateful for, that I see."

" Not for all that you did for me—for all that you haf done for me always ? " said Lizette, looking up with her eyes bright with excitement into the astonished grey-green ones. " I was thinking ever so much of all you haf done for me, Jerry, and that I haf never said enough thank you. I want to say it now, for you haf been very good to me."

" Oh, that's all nonsense," blundered out Jerry, saying, of course, the very thing he did not mean. " That is, I didn't do no more yesterday than I have done always. I mean that I didn't do any more then than I'd do for anybody."

If he had not fortunately, but secretly much to his own annoyance, blushed crimson and looked exactly as if he were answering some charge of great weight respecting his character, his listener might have believed what he said.

As it was, she was just beginning to understand this big fellow, or thought she was, so she smiled back at him, and proceeded to add to his confusion by saying,—

" Guardian angels and brothers deserve a reward when they are more good than is usual. I
go to give to you something, Jerry."

" Give me something ! " repeated Jerry. " Now
don't you get wasting your money on me, Liz ;
you've 'none to spare, in spite of the time you
spend over those faldals and things."

" But, for all you say, I am going to give
something to you. Do not be afraid; it will not
be something extravagant. I am poor, but I can
afford this. It is not paid for with the money."

" Not bought with money."

" No. I will you to guess."

" Oh, I am such a lubber," began Jerry, using
a new term to describe his stupidity. " I should
never guess."

But still he was bidden try, and did not make
such a very big blunder at starting after all.

Although not as a rule what might exactly be
called sentimental, he had a desire to possess
nothing but one of those same roses with which
the breeze had played the night before.

" One of my roses," said Lizette, touching them
caressingly. " No ; that is not what I will give
you. I cannot lose them."

" Then I give it up," replied Jerry, not ventur-
ing a second attempt.

" Well, then, I suppose I must tell it to you. I
was thinking all about you last night, and I
wanted to seek a way to say I am happy for what
that you did for me ; and I thought, ' He is my
brother '—is it not so ? " Jerry nodded. " Yes,

he is my brother—it would be like a sister to—to give to him a kiss."

Ah, Lizette, Lizette, how is it you so little understand the lesson of the roses. Do not laugh at her, dear reader, she had not found the truth yet. She did not know, or rather comprehend, what was in her heart.

Had the earth opened and shown him all its secrets, the effect upon our hero which this proposal made could not have been greater. His face became suddenly crimson ; his eyes drooped from the frankly upturned gaze to the floor; and for several moments he could only stand hopelessly confused and speechless. His heart was beating wildly under his rough smoke-coloured coat—there was a big lump in his throat—and the perspiration stood out on his forehead.

And all this because his little sister had offered him a kiss—a tribute of affection which any brother might, nay, had a right to expect. If ever in his life Jerry was afraid of himself it was then. He was afraid lest after all he should lose in one moment what he had so nearly gained by long weary days of strife,—lest he should forget the vow by which he was bound,—forget that soft voice called him " brother,"—forget everything but the love in his heart which had never seen the light—the love which that sisterly kiss would seal down for ever.

The struggle was a severe one. A little more and the words he had hidden so long in his heart would have burst forth, and brother and sisterhood would have been impossible. A little more —but— He looked down at the frank girlish face, still bearing the trace of the blow under which she had fallen for her love's face—to his ears came back the memory of the broken song in the mother tongue, and he paused. A moment and all was over. The battle won.

But he would not dare trust himself to feel upon his cheek those soft lips, still warm with the kisses of the love she loved—the only love she ever would love.

" I would rather have the rose, Liz," he said, so quietly that the girl looked curiously at him, quite at a loss to understand the strange look in his face. She understood only too well afterwards. " I would rather have the rose," adding, with a lame attempt to speak lightly, " It will last."

Lizette did not seem to mind his preference.

" Then it is the rose which you shall haf. Choose." And she took the blossoms from her bosom and held them to him.

" I'd rather you did for me," said Jerry, afraid lest his hand should not be quite steady. What a big coward he was, to be sure.

So Lizette chose for him, picking out from among the rest the very bud which had so nearly withered in the night. She stood up, and, looking laughingly into his face, fastened it into his coat.

" There," she said triumphantly, " you look quite—what is it?—handsome."

As she spoke, and while yet she stood close beside him, her fingers touching his coat, the door opened, and in blundered Sarah. She had knocked twice and received no answer, so, supposing the room was empty, had gone in. Seeing who it was, Lizette called gaily to her to admire her handiwork, and Jerry summoned up enough presence of mind to make some laughing comment.

To their united surprise the girl, instead of giving back some queer reply and lingering on her errand, put down the parcel she carried, and blundered out of the room with more speed than she usually used.

"What is gone to be the way with her?" said Lizette, looking after her in astonishment.

"I expect 'Missus has been a-giving it to her again,' as she calls it. Poor wretch, she has a time of it, with the immortal 'Sarah! Sarah!'"

"I have pity for her," replied Lizette softly. "She is one of the friends who have been good for me."

"What, is she a brick and a guardian angel too?" And the two fell to laughing at the silly nonsense, like two happy children.

A little later Jerry said good-bye, promising to come again later in the day. When he reached the hall he found Sarah there making a pretence of dusting the hat-stand, but in reality doing more damage to the hats and umbrellas it supported than made the operation at all a desirable one. Seeing Jerry, she opened the front door for him to pass. This unwonted civility on her part called forth a comment from Jerry. Again his remark was received with anything but good-nature.

"Get along, will you?" replied the slavey, motioning him roughly towards the door. "Don't you see you're in my way?"

This was far from true, but knowing and sympathising with the aggravation consequent upon that everlasting call "Sarah!" Jerry took her broad hint and moved on.

No sooner was he on the doorstep than Sarah banged the door to after him with great and unnecessary violence. As she did so, Mrs Spicer made her appearance from the lower regions, and in a few minutes was in full swing of that oft-repeated operation, "giving it" to her handmaid. Usually, the contest was entirely a one-sided one, but on this occasion, urged on by some impulse for which I cannot account, Sarah "gave as good as she took;" indeed, worked herself up to such a pitch of excitement, that in emphasising a statement more remarkable for the earnestness with which it was uttered than correctness of grammar or construction, she restored a well-worn beaver to its peg with such force as to knock a good-sized hole in the crown.

As it happened, the topper was only a relic of a departed parlour-boarder—all he had left to pay six months' rent, when he completely and unexpectedly vanished from the scene of action, and had been hung by his defrauded landlady in a prominent

position, as a sort of trophy of vengeance,—a sort
of reminder—if she needed any—henceforth never
to place any trust in lodgers—much less man.

Judging, however, from the wrath poured upon
the unlucky servant in consequence of her carelessness, one might at least have imagined she
had wilfully destroyed some family heirloom.
The discussion which had been the cause of her
excitement came to an abrupt conclusion, and the
usual one-sided one, superseded it. Judging from
the quiet way in which the unfortunate " slavey "
listened to the aspersions on her own character,
one was led to believe that for once she and her
shortcomings had not been the object of the first
battle.

Meanwhile Jerry went slowly on his way homeward, not giving another thought to the servant's
rather strange manner. He was used to her
queerness by this time, and excused it all for the
sake of her kindness, rough and ready as it was,
to his little sister.

No, his thoughts were too much occupied with
that little scene in which he had received the rose
he wore in his coat, to have time for anything
else. Over and over again he rehearsed it to himself, sometimes thinking he had acted rightly—
sometimes wrongly.

Had he been cold in refusing the kiss so frankly
offered? Had he been ill-advised not to receive
the gift in the way it had been proffered—a gift
which would have been so precious to him? The
questions each in turn received its answer, but

the latter one recurred the more often. Now that the danger was over, it did not seem half so great; indeed, Jerry quite blamed himself for being prudish, stupid, nay, even unkind, for having acted as he did.

He arrived at this conclusion just as he reached his lodgings, where in the hall he again found someone in waiting for him. This was Miss Withers, whom lately, owing to his state of mind, like Lizette's, having been somewhat more cheerful than formerly, he had treated so affably that she grew daily more and more fascinated, and more determined in her attempts to waylay his affections. In order to effect this, she practised, as we know, the same operation upon him, in person; indeed, the manœuvres which she had gone through during the few past weeks, in order to gain her cause, were truly laughable. Her friends were kept well informed of the whole matter, and whether from any colouring given by the lady, it is impossible to say—but certain it is that the affair was supposed to be in that satisfactory state in which the former one had been—that is, before Jerry had selected the happy Jane from among a numerous audience—to take a card.

On the morning, however, in question, the adoring heart of this young female received a slight repulse. She had espied her (supposed) admirer, as she frequently did, when he was some distance up the street, and straightway descended into the hall to await his coming. The moment he laid his hand upon the knocker, she opened the door with a suddenness which nearly precipitated her into his arms, a contingency which, in our hero's frame of mind, was anything but desirable.

Jane blushed—however she managed the flush so often is a miracle—and murmured something about the lock of the door needing oiling. Jerry, none too sweetly, a wonder for him, but all because of the dissatisfaction which he felt at his own conduct concerning the proffered kiss, replied that he wished the young lady would perform the necessary operation, and let him have a key, so that he could let himself in.

The moment he had spoken so irritatedly, his usual good temper made him thoroughly ashamed of himself, and he at once began to make atonement. Now Jane had had experience enough to enable her to manage such an affair as this with skill. She therefore looked upon this change of mood in her aunt's lodger as a most favourable sign, and withheld pardon for his crossness for at least a quarter of an hour, during which time she managed to sigh and languish and gush a great deal, and draw from him a lot of small talk (very small on his part), to which process he submitted rather more readily than usual, owing to his having so nearly lost his temper but a short time before.

At the end of fifteen minutes he was able by an effort to make his escape, and at once put the entire incident out of his head.

Not so the lady. Either she was slightly deaf, or wilfully misunderstood what had passed during the *tête-à-tête* in the hall ; but certainly the report she gave of it to her bosom friend, Miss Mary Saunders, when she paid her a visit that same evening, was not, strictly speaking, an accurate one. Could Jerry only have overheard how his blunt speeches were twisted and turned into any meaning but the one which he intended them to convey, he would have at once transported himself bag and baggage from the neighbourhood of such a designing young female as Jane Withers.

For the next few days that young lady was in a perfect flutter of excitement, and paid a good many visits to her friends, to all of whom, as to Miss Saunders, she told some great secret, at which each in turn was very pleased, and seemed to offer their visitor as many good wishes as if it were Christmas Day, New Year's Day, and a birthday rolled into one.

At the end of a week Miss Jane received an intimation from her seamstress that the last of her friend's order was finished, awaiting her approval.

Lately the young lady had contented herself with merely sending and fetching work by the errand-boy, a course which Jerry had himself proposed ; for it will already have been guessed that it was Lizette's brother who had devised this scheme for aiding her. But on this occasion Miss Jane having been commissioned by "her friend," as she, with much *empressement*, called this mysterious being, to settle the account, she, in company with Miss Saunders, paid a visit to Mrs Spicer's third-floor front, and interviewed the little seamstress. But before this visit took place, a change had once more come over the complexion of things with regard to my hero and heroine, those of the latter particularly.

It happened that later on in the day of his oft-detailed conversation with his landlady's niece, Jerry, as usual, turned his steps once more in the direction of Mrs Spicer's. By this time his constant visits had made him well known among the lodgers, with whom he was held in no little favour, in consequence of the supposed devotion to his invalid sister. Often when passing out or in he would stop and have a chat now with one, now with another, of the different "floors." When, therefore, on reaching the first landing, he met Lizette's nearest neighbour—the third floor back—a sad-faced woman, who did some work at a theatre somewhere in the neighbourhood — one of those haunted-looking creatures whose histories are the secrets of the big city, Jerry nodded cheerily to her, and made some light remark, such as had been on his lips all day, I suppose because of that sort of air-tight feeling which he had had in his breast.

Although usually acknowledged by her neighbours to be anything but sociable in disposition, the woman usually responded to his overtures of friendship—his frank manner won its way with her as with many others. But on this occasion she hastened rather than slackened her steps, and answered his remark very briefly, turning her head away, as if she wished to avoid notice.

"Poor thing," thought Jerry, whistling softly
as he went on his way; "she's in trouble again,
I suppose," adding some unexpressed thought
relative to a wish that he might expand his
heart and pocket in order to be able to extend
his protection farther than he did at present.
"Ah," smiling and muttering softly to himself
as he made this reservation in his good nature,
"he did not mind how far the brotherhood was
extended, but he would never have but one little
sister." There is no need to say who was the
one he had in his mind.

His thoughts on this subject were interrupted
by his meeting, a few steps further on, a young
fellow who was the occupant of the dismal garret
which Lizette had formerly occupied; a queer-
looking sort of customer, and one who was regarded by the rest of the lodgers with suspicion
and distrust. He seemed to be a lazy loafer—
if the truth had been known, up to very little
good—but as he kept himself to himself in a way
which was at the same time anything but frank
and openhanded, as yet no actual cause for com-
plaint had been found against him.

He was distinctly avoided by his neighbours,—
even beneath the notice of the top floor—the chain
of acquaintance between the basement and roof
being thus broken. He did not seem to mind
being in Coventry in the least; on the contrary,
when Jerry, passing him on the stairs one day,
happened to push against him and good-naturedly
begged his pardon, following up the introduction

by a nod or greeting if they chanced to meet, all he got in return was a surly grunt or growl.

On the day, however, of which I write, the "attic" was the first to make any sign of recognition—a sulky sort of a grin.

Jerry returned it, attaching no special importance to the circumstance at the time, and continued on his way. On the next landing he met Madame Petite. He greeted her cheerily, and made some laughing remark as to how she had left his little sister after her exertions of the day before—then suddenly broke off his merry tone, and asked quickly and anxiously if anything was amiss.

At first the little Frenchwoman evaded his inquiry; but it was easy to tell by her face that something was amiss. It had on it that worried look which to those who knew her best meant that matters were not smooth with her.

Jerry was fearful lest this might have to do with Lizette,—lest the exertion of the day before had after all proved too much for her; but a few words set these fears at rest—but only, alas! to raise others.

For some little time the two stood talking earnestly on the landing—at least Madame Petite told what her trouble was, and our hero listened, with a rather disturbed look creeping into his face, in the place of the light-hearted one which it had so lately worn. He did not say much; but silence on his part, we know, meant that he thought the more.

That evening, although we have seen him so far on his journey—only, in fact, a few steps from her door—Lizette had no visit from her brother. She had not seen him come in, having been bidding Madame Petite good-bye, after vainly trying to understand what was the matter with her—what her trouble—so did not know of the meeting on the stairs, after which the little Frenchwoman and Jerry left the house together, parting at the end of the street— the former to make her way to the Hall of Varieties with as much speed as she could muster —the latter to go by a more round-about way, and with certainly a slower step and graver face than usual. That evening the watcher at the window waited in vain; and the evening seemed very long and dreary.

The next day, too, instead of appearing as usual, Jerry sent a note telling of his accidental meeting with a friend who lived at the other end of the town, and who had invited him to pass a few days with him, which invitation had been accepted. The note was very offhand—indeed, singular in tone, which singularity puzzled Lizette not a little.

She read and re-read the short epistle many times, then folded it up and placed it in her workbox with a little sigh, only the next moment to take it out, tear it with seemingly unnecessary haste into a dozen pieces, and throw it into the fireplace. At first she stretched out her hand to let the fragments fall out of the window, but changed her mind, and dropped them softly into the fender. This done, she went on industriously with her work for some little time, turning her head every now and then to look out into the street below, for she was once more sitting in the sunlight, the blind kitten curled up in her lap. This action of hers must have been purely force of habit. She had evidently forgotten she had no visitor to expect that day.

She evidently *had* forgotten this, and every time she remembered it she returned to her work, not always, I am bound to say, with increasing ardour. Indeed, after a little, she who had lately sat at her task with not a little perseverance, after repeatedly indulging in this distraction, seemed to become unusually languid, laid down her needle, and sat looking absently out the window.

In a few minutes she roused herself, and again took up her work, worked quickly away for a few minutes, and then looked round, this time not out of the window, but in the direction of the fireplace. As she did so—as if tired of the silence, and eager for some voice—even her own—to break the monotony and direct her thoughts—she said aloud, bending over the kitten, perhaps expecting sympathy from even its small presence, " It is lonely, Whispy, isn't it ? It is sad to be here all alone. We have not any friends to-day; they have got tired of us. Is it not so ? Ah, well ! we must not to be greedy. They have been good. It is play now, and we will not be sorry of it, will we ? Pleasure is good after that we have worked, and

we will be content. He—my friend, who wills
that you sit on his shoulder, Whispy—has to go
to be with his other friends, and we will be glad,
is it not? Yes, we will be glad." And the thin
white hands closed caressingly over the little ball
of grey fur, and the kitten rubbed its fluffy head
against the tapering fingers, offering what comfort it could.

I suppose, although English born, by this time
the kitten was well versed in the " gibberish," as
Jerry called it, for Lizette always spoke in her
own beloved language when she had any special
thoughts to express. " Yes," she went on softly,
" we will be glad, if our good friend is happy. He
is kind and good, he ought to have pleasure sometimes. And it can be none for him to come here,
so we will be glad. But," in a lower whisper, " it
will be lonely without him. Yes, very lonely.
Only you and me, Whispy. No one else—no
brother, not for ever so long. We shall be lonely."

There was a touch of the old sadness in her
voice which had so long been absent from it, as if
her brother, gone from her for even so short a
time, made her life seem very dreary. Had he
not brought all the sunshine into it? Now he was
gone, it was little wonder so timid a young spirit
should miss his coming—his quick firm step on the
stair, his cheery greeting, his pleasant smile, his
thoughtful little gifts which, when he had gone,
seemed doubly precious, his never-failing goodness, and, what was even better, his ever-constant
cheerfulness, his—in fact, himself, in thought,

word, and deed—all were missed now that they were gone.

A few days was not long; but to Lizette, I suppose, because of her loneliness, it seemed an eternity.

I wish, she thought to herself, that he had said some definite time. It would be nice to know when to expect him. A few days may mean two or three or more. He might have said how long. And he might have come and said good-bye. It was unkind of him not to say good-bye. This thought had been in her mind some time, and had at last struggled out. And now that it had done so, she was rather ashamed of it than otherwise. "Unkind! Jerry unkind! What an ungrateful, selfish girl I am getting, to want to deprive him of his pleasure. He who has been so kind, so good to me. It is I who am unkind, not he. I hope he will enjoy his holiday. And we—we, Whispy, must enjoy ourselves, at least we will try; but," with a little sigh, returning to her first idea, "it will be very lonely." And so she found it. Although Jerry's visits had only occupied a very small portion of the day, the remembrance of them must have lasted far longer, for the lonely feeling extended over nearly all the little seamstress's waking hours, and the white kitten was the recipient of an amount of information which, had it been a cat of very remarkable sagacity, might have given it a clue to the true state of affairs.

As it was, it only purred, rubbed its fluffy head round its mistress's neck, and kept its opinion of the matter to itself. Perhaps it was because she knew that not even its eyes could look into her own and read in them what she hardly knew herself, that Lizette so fearlessly confided in it. But in spite of this little scrap of comfort, the days seemed very long. Strangely enough, too, when she "did" the room on the day following the receipt of the young clown's letter, Sarah found no scraps of paper in the fireplace. I suppose Lizette had been seized with another tidying fit, and perhaps disposed of the fragments of the torn letter as she had at first intended.

So the few days crept slowly along, and the little German girl expected in vain. Nearly a week went by, and still she was left to be lonely and sad—for sad she was, restless and discontented, scarcely knowing why — hoping for a letter, a message, some news of any sort, some sign, but none came.

And where was Jerry all this time? Who was this suddenly discovered friend for whom he had forsaken his little sister, just when she was beginning to find out his true worth? Who was he? Why, a creature of the young clown's imagination, which same not being by any means a vivid one, had seen no other way out of the difficulty in which he found himself than in this creation.

When Lizette imagined him enjoying himself with his friend, he was in fact in no other place than his old lodgings, enjoying a sort of self-inflicted solitary confinement. There was no reason why he should not have gone about his business as usual. Lizette, being a prisoner, would never have known of his whereabouts, provided he avoided Wicker's Row. But this, if once he set off on a ramble, he found himself unable to do. On the first day of his singular behaviour, he had decided to pass the time by making acquaintance with the other end of the town. Accordingly he started with the determination of going for a good long tramp, which might help him to disperse the blue devils, from a fit of which he had been suffering during that day and part of the former one. He walked resolutely in the direction he had planned, for about half-an-hour, then, although as a rule a good pedestrian, grew tired, and decided to rest a bit. This he did, and again set off on his way, only soon to yield once more to the feeling of tiredness. He rested again, and this time decided to turn his steps by a round-about way homewards. He kept to this intention for a short while, but at last gave up any idea but that of returning the shortest way possible, which way led, in fact, down Wicker's Row—the very place of all others which he wished to avoid. I do not think he was aware how little control he had over his inclination, until he found himself in the act of turning the corner of the street. Then he came to a full stop, pulled himself together, and set off to his lodgings, vowing vengeance on himself for his stupidity.

So while Lizette was so devoutly wishing he

were enjoying his holiday, and yet wishing she was able to look forward to his coming, imagining him miles away, he was in reality but a few yards away from her, wanting very much to run in, if only for a few minutes, to see how his little sister fared, divided from her by a gulf to which all along he had been trying to shut his eyes, and which now by a turn—a backward one, it would appear—of fortune's wheel, was suddenly opened under his very feet.

It was to avoid this abyss that he had gone to all this trouble of invention, an art in which he had had very little practice, so no wonder his attempts were rather feeble ones.

By an effort he succeeded in saving himself from ruining his scheme at the very commencement, namely, by turning his steps in a reverse direction to that in which his inclination would have led him. He went home a sadder but a wiser man, glad to have conquered, but very weary and worn with the struggle.

It had been the same old one—old, but yet none the less vigorous in strength, even now as fierce as when he had first fought it — the struggle between self and love.

CHAPTER VII.

JERRY'S BANISHMENT.

THE following day Jerry stayed indoors, save for his excursions to and from the show, during which he had to exercise a sort of mental policemanship over his will, lest he should be in any way led astray. He was, so far, able to hold himself in check; but when on the next day, tired of his seclusion, and beginning to find it had an alarming effect upon his spirits, he repeated the experiment in the form of a second ramble, and only once again saved himself from acting, as he said, "like a fool and an idiot."

This failure proved to him that "banishment and nought but banishment" would answer his purpose. Hence the solitary confinement. He did not know what course he was going to take when this supposed visit to his supposed friend was over. He had said it would be for a few days, hoping by that time that he would have hit upon some plan, but he saw a whole week go by without any ray of light gleaming upon his mental darkness.

All this time he kept himself well aware of Lizette's wellbeing by means of a small "odd jobs" boy whom Mrs Spicer employed. This boy, by means of sundry bribes, interested himself greatly in the third-floor front, about whom Sarah never seemed loath to talk. Through this "artful youth" Jerry was able to trace the widening of the gulf which lay between him and the poor seamstress,—to watch the trail of the train which the jockey's hand had lighted. Its progress was slow but sure—the "secret" spreading from floor to floor—beginning, strangely enough, at the top, where dwelt the questionable-charactered young man. In a little it could not help but reach the fountain head of the establishment's respectability—the parlours. When this should happen, as Sarah said, there would be a grand "bust up;" which I suppose meant that Mrs Spicer would be induced to take some course by which to save the character of her establishment. Meanwhile she preserved strict neutrality. And all this time, while the mine was being fired, what of Lizette?

She alone, the chief actor in the pitiful drama, knew nothing of what was going on around her. She was innocent of any attempt to do wrong, and never guessed that others should deem her otherwise.

Yes, she knew nothing. While those around her were busy clacking their tongues, and, in virtuous indignation, pointing fingers of scorn at her, all ready to cast the stones which none had truly any right to throw, she had no deeper feeling in her heart than that of loneliness, of longing for the company of that cheery, brave fellow who was slowly, although she knew it not, lifting her—the crushed, bruised flower—out of the darkness into the sunlight once more.

It was hard that when the dawn was so near the clouds should gather again.

A few days. How long they seemed! Would they never end? Yes, they were long, but in them, although the harvest-time was yet far off, the tiny seeds which were to bear such fulsome blossoms were being sown in the wounded heart —blossoms whose gentle growth had first to be checked by those stones of circumstance and slander which were being cast upon them.

At last the week came to an end. Now, surely, the waiting days were over. Surely he will come to-day ; yes, surely he will come to-day!

Such were Lizette's thoughts on waking on the morning which counted a whole week since that last time she had seen her " brother." The thought had been almost her first for nearly every day since he had gone without saying good-bye. But this morning it seemed to be more sure, more certain ; and somehow with the conviction that that day he would come, the gloom and loneliness of the last few days seemed to begin to roll away. It needed only " his " coming to disperse both entirely. Lizette did not know this. It was too soon. The seeds were not yet even quickened. No—that was to come.

But first there was the stones, the trampling feet, the scorching sun of malice, which knows not the evil from the good.

All the morning of that day on which she had said so assuredly and hopefully, "He will come to-day," Lizette was as blythe and busy as a bee.

Stitch—stitch—stitch—the needle flew in and out. But there was no sadness or weariness in the picture this little seamstress made ; instead, a sort of indescribable hopefulness, which was strangely unlike the dreariness which had gradually become part of the past.

All the morning she sat at her task, with an energy which was a contrast to her listlessness in days gone by. Mid-day came at last, and without bringing any visitor.

She said to herself, for the hope was very strong within her,—" He will come this afternoon. He would know how busy I am in the morning."

And then she stitched bravely away till dinner time. The meal which Sarah brought her she ate quickly, like one in a hurry to start for a journey. During those few days Sarah had altered greatly in her manner. She who had formerly been so taciturn and silent, seemed to have taken quite a different attitude. It was as if at last some influence had touched her rough character and softened her unconsciously. She would sometimes stay and chat quite sociably with the kitten's mistress—offered her help in many little ways,—in fact was—now that to an outsider it would have appeared too late—everything which the doctor had tried to make her long before.

The cause of the change it is easy to guess. It is often from those from whom we least expect sympathy that we receive it, when the rest of the world turns coldly from us.

Sarah knew that ere long the "secret" which was known to so many would bear its fruit, and in her blundering way she was trying to show that here at least was one who did not believe the tales which were afloat.

Believe! She believe those ugly whispers! There was no need to ask the question. If her manner did not speak for itself, at least there was that muttered whisper which day after day she repeated, after any interview with Lizette,—

"I don't believe it. It's all a pack of lies, and I've a very good mind to up and tell them so," she would say.

But beyond, by way of emphasis, breaking one or two articles of fragile make in thus expressing her opinion, she made no further stand against the evil. Perhaps to atone for her unusual gentleness when with Lizette, or perhaps because of the equally unusual disturbed state of her thoughts, Mrs Spicer's list of "breakages" to be deducted from her wages, made pay-day for Sarah, at least, a mockery.

This did not tend to calm her excitement. She persisted in her resolute "I don't believe it," uttering the same at odd times. She did so on the day in question with more vehemence than usual, when, early in the afternoon, she found occasion, as she often did now, to run into the third-floor front, to see how its inhabitant was "getting along," as she phrased it.

Lizette, although it was not a holiday—why should it be!—was in holiday trim, dressed with even more care than on that same day a week before. The grey dress, brightened by knots of rosy ribbons—one placed among the fast-growing curls—a mode of decoration which she had not used before, because it reminded her of the old days, and which suited her well, a white rose at her throat, the rest in a vase on the table beside her, and her needle flying in and out faster and still faster.

She had flung the window wide open—for the air was very warm, the sun pouring down with great force, and a grey look in the west, which to the weather meant mischief before long—and drawn her chair close to it, as if eager to catch every breath of the cool, refreshing breeze—every warm sunbeam, which came from without. The flush in her face was more distinct than ever, her eyes bright and clear, and her whole face full of a sunny happiness which was fast giving it back its old beauty.

She was singing, too—this time in English—some pretty little ballad, which sounded doubly sweet in her broken words. She was not now afraid that anyone might overhear her. Every now and then she would glance down the street as though expecting someone, and then go on working faster

than before, as if she were sewing into her task
the moments which seemed so long in passing.
When Sarah entered the room, her needle was
still for a moment, and she had rested her head
back in the chair, lost in thought. The sunshine
was touching her face and hair softly—almost
caressingly, the scarred cheek hidden by her
hand, and the golden brown curls forming as of
old a clustering halo round her forehead. Sarah
must have entered the room more softly than
was her wont, for she had stood for some moments looking stolidly at her little friend, thinking, in her dull way, that, in spite of all that
slanderous tongues were saying, she whom they
called by a very ugly name,—unfit to live beneath
the same roof as honest people (*i.e.*, this does not
include the young man in the attics), was sweeter
and fairer to look upon than those models of pro-
priety on the lower floors.

I think she dimly realised just then that there
was some transformation gradually going on in
this strange little invalid—a transformation which
made the gathering clouds seem all the more
cruel and gloomy in their darkness.

"I don't believe it," she said, half aloud, for
once forgetting the injunction which of her own
free will she had laid upon herself—namely, not
to be the first one to set the ball rolling to the
foot of the hill; "I don't believe it!"

At the sound of her voice breaking the silence,
Lizette started up from her reverie, half unconsciously rising to her feet, the warm glow of colour

in her face deepening suddenly, the name of him who had been in her thoughts almost on her lips.

It did not, however, pass them. She sat down quickly, with the colour fading slowly out of her face—perhaps from disappointment that her day-dream was not reality.

Then, as Sarah still stared at her with the solemnity of a great white owl, the faint shadow of the pretty dimples which had once been there played round her mouth as she smiled brightly—a gay, sunny smile which took Sarah by surprise, but would have been valued beyond anything by some one else—it was so like one of those which the little fancy rider was wont to bestow in return for any kindness in those days gone by—and said gaily,—

"What is it you see in me to make you look so, Sarah? Is it that I am altered since that you saw me last?"

"Since I saw yer last! Why, it's only an hour ago. (I'd have been up before," apologetically, "but the parlours took such a time over their dinners.) Altered since then! You're a-laughing, Miss Lizet."

At this Lizette did laugh in real earnest. Sarah joined in, rubbing her big greasy hands up and down her apron by way of accompaniment to the chuckling sound by which she expressed her merriment.

And I do not believe if you had asked either of them why they laughed, that they would have been able to tell you. I believe the true reason was, that both felt irresistibly happy—the one

because it seemed no use—no good to be otherwise, because I don't think she could quite help it—
the other, because she was glad her friend was so.

At last Lizette grew sober—at least as near to
solemn as it was possible for her to be just then.

"I think you rude—very, indeed rude Sarah,"
she said, with an attempt at dignity which did
not at all agree with the still dancing dimples.

"Me—rude! Lor' now, Miss Lizet, what hever
'ave I done?"

"Done! Why, have you not make the most of
rude remarks about me?"

"Why, I didn't say nothing!"

"No, but you have the thought, and you look
it. It is very rude."

"Lor' miss, 'ow quick you do read a body's
thoughts; not as how I thought much,—only as
how you 'looked a bit spry,' just as if how yer
was expecting yer sweetheart."

Lizette returned the look of admiration with
one of equal candour, and said with a half smile,
half sigh, the former predominating,—"I have no
sweetheart, Sarah," adding, with a touch of that
sorrow in her voice which made her seem all the
more a child,—"I have no sweetheart, Sarah: I
am not pretty enough."

"Lor' it ain't only the pretty girls as gets
chaps to take notice of 'em. Why, there's Polly
Flanders along the Row took up with by one of
them 'ere gents from the circus at the 'All of
Varieties, and she's ugly enough in all conscience
—not that you're plain, as you will try and make

yourself out. Folks don't usually look up to much when they've been shut up in a hole like this so long as you 'ave. I won't say you 'ave, but I do say as how now yer a-beginning to get about a bit, I do say as how you're beginning to look mighty different to what you were. That 'ere dress is better 'n the old dingy black 'un (I'd rip the other up, if I was you,—make a petticoat of it), and them 'ere ribbons is just nobby" (whatever that may mean). " Why don't yer always 'fig'" (another word of rather obscure meaning) " yourself out like this always? It'd be better for yer, I'm thinking; ye're looking as spry as can be; and when yer hair grows, and yer has more going out than just now, I guess you'll be fine—won't you now? "

Lizette laughed in childish glee, and touched the bright ribbons she wore caressingly with her fingers, with a look on her face which moved Sarah to touch the short golden brown curls softly with her big, coarse hand.

She did not speak, but there was a queer expression in her eyes, as if she was trying to make out some idea which had just entered her mind— I suppose dragged in by the previous one. So brilliant was this last, that it was some moments before she could put it into words. Then she began with strangely enough a contrary statement to that which had so often been on her lips lately.

"Lawks bless us and save us, I do believe as how—"

She got no further. The cry of "Sarah! Sarah!" in some alarming proximity, advised her of the nearness of her mistress. The sentence which would have told Lizette so much—everything in fact that just then there was to tell her—ended in the usual "I'm a-coming—I'm a-coming."

Lizette was left alone once more. She sat for a few moments listening to the sound of the girl's departing footsteps, then with a swift step she crossed the room, and reached down the little cracked looking-glass from where it hung, and carried it to the window.

Don't be angry with her, dear reader, and call her vain and foolish for loving to be fair and pretty to look upon. It was not for herself that she cared.

Before, however, she could take more than one peep,—catch sight of more than a face bright with the glow of returning health and happiness; there was again a sound of footsteps on the stairs. She hastily laid the glass aside, and with a smile of welcome—a little half-suppressed cry, she sprang to the door — to meet Miss Jane Withers and her friend come to settle the account.

Well, well—duty first and pleasure afterwards.

. . . .

The duty lasted fully half-an-hour. Miss Jane, it would appear, took rather a fancy to the little seamstress, who was so gay and chatty. The young lady was, I think, rather in the mood to be pleased with any chance acquaintance, any one, in fact, who would listen to the "secret" which she was so ready to impart with so much smiling, gushing, and smirking. In this case, too, she had an aider and abetter in the shape of her bosom friend, who, in the most charming manner in the world, drew from her the recital, occupying as it were the post of interpreter, adding her own comments and ideas on the subject, which certainly did not tend to relieve them of any colouring.

After hinting and giggling for some time, speaking a great deal of a certain "him" who was evidently a very happy man, Lizette, as she laid the dainty work on a sheet of brown paper preparatory to folding it up in a parcel, made some remark in reference to his name.

"My love is a ——, and his name begins with a J," said the bosom friend, with an attempt at friskiness.

"Oh, hush," said Miss Jane, looking at once pleased and shy.

"I'll be as silent as the grave," was the joking reply. "Not a living soul shall know from my lips that J stands for—"

Here ensued a slight scuffle between the ladies, during which, by way of revenge, the "friend" managed to impart in a loud whisper to Lizette the desired information, whereupon further playful altercation took place, in which the little seamstress seemed to take great interest, for she stood by the table looking from one to the other of the two squabblers, holding the string and paper in either hand, without going on with her business of tying it up.

It would seem, too, that she soon tired of the silly nonsense, for she only asked one question, to which she received an answer of some length from the communicative bosom friend. This answer related several passages in the life of a circus clown, which I think would rather have surprised him could he have heard them. At any rate, they surprised some one. Some of them, indeed, were so astonishing that the disclosure of how he had spent those last "few days" was of very small account.

After this Lizette tied up the parcel. Rather carelessly, it would appear ; for when the "happy lady" and her friend reached home and inspected in secret the "faldals" before handing them over to the rightful owner (only a matter of form this, as was whispered, such a pretty way to manage an affair of the sort), they found the string had been tied so tightly that it needed to be cut, and the paper twisted so close that the lace and ribbons were sadly creased. I suppose the little seamstress was so interested in what she heard concerning her employer's approaching nuptials that she did not notice what she was doing.

Miss Jane Withers remarked that she had thought the sewing girl rather a bright, pretty little thing at first. She did not say whether she had altered that opinion, and if so, why.

. . . .

And while the two friends sat after walking home through the heat, and talked over, with more giggling and gushing, the future which was entirely of their own planning—the hero in the drama all unconscious of the part which they had assigned to him—how was this same little seamstress faring? Was she still sitting in the sunlight singing songs of happiness, with that look of joy on her face?

No, the picture she now presented was rather like one belonging to the past—that dreary vista of dead hope—than to the present, which so lately had seemed so bright.

After her visitors had left her, she had sat quietly down in her chair, and looked round her with a strange bewildered look on her face.

Presently she began to repeat some words over to herself, as if their meaning was hard to comprehend. Then she rose suddenly, and crossing, leant out the window; but the sunshine no longer found any reflection in her eyes. She put her hand to her forehead and pushed her hair back with trembling fingers, while her teeth met over her lips as if she were in pain. The colour had slowly faded from her cheeks, and her breath came and went quickly.

For a little she waited to let the breeze fan her cheeks, but the air was still—no breath of wind came to her relief. Then her glance fell upon the little mirror which she had laid aside. Steadying herself by the curtain, she stretched out her hand and took it up, standing so that the sunlight, which seemed suddenly to have lost its warmth and gold—to have become pale and cold as noonlight—fell upon her.

For the brief space of a moment she looked down at the reflection the glass bore. How changed from that of a short half-hour before. The bright face of a child of unconscious happiness was gone—in its place the white, wan one of the girl who had been "so lonely with no one to love her"—in the days gone by—the face of one who had been confronted with some great truth—too great to be realised all at once.

A moment the dull haggard eyes gazed on the scarred countenance—the scar showing with double clearness against the pallor—till suddenly they met the glance of those in the glass.

An instant—the look which told all was returned—then, letting the glass fall to the table, Lizette fell upon her knees by the window, hiding her face in the curtains, which, by a strange, uncontrollable impulse, she had drawn over the window, shutting out the sunlight.

Down, down, she crouched down, not wildly as she had once done when in grief, but slowly, like one who sinks under a heavy load. And there, kneeling alone in the shadow, she whispered, with every drop of blood in her body burning her cheeks, "I offered to kiss him; oh, why have I been so blind!"

Presently she started up and pulled aside the curtains again. A change had come over the world, it seemed, in those few moments. How close it was—the still air seemed full of sultriness. Not a breath of wind was stirring. The sky had gone grey and sullen, the sunlight was gone; in its place a sort of lurid haze, which dazzled the eyes and scorched the dusty pavement. The people in the street below looked up anxiously at the sky, and hurried on their way as fast as the stupefying heat would let them. Lizette leant far out the window, but no coolness was to be found. Suddenly she moved across the room, lifted down a shawl and a little black hat from a nail behind the door. The white fleecy wrapper and pretty hat lay unheeded on a chair. She was going out —out into the air: the atmosphere of the house seemed as if it would choke her.

She passed down the stairs without meeting a soul, for Sarah and Mrs Spicer were engaged in that most important of all lodging operations— the concoction of tea for the parlours—and slipping quietly out of the street door, closed it quietly behind her.

She had no idea where she was going, no thought as to whether her strength would carry her, only a wish to get away from the house. At any moment he for whom all day she had been watching might come, and she could not face him. No, not yet.

She walked resolutely, even quickly, down the street in the opposite direction to that in which her visitor might be expected to come.

At the corner she met her fellow lodger, the young man from the attics, lounging along in his usual dilatory fashion. He stared fixedly at her— for, unlike when starting for her expedition on her birthday, she had not thought of putting on a veil, and her white features, on which the scar showed more plainly than ever, attracted his attention—and then nodded familiarly, and half paused, as if to address her.

But she drew away from him and passed on quickly in the glare, which was momentarily growing duller and duller, while, although the traffic in the road was the same, the noise of it all—at least to Lizette's ears—was deadened, muffled.

She hurried on in her aimless errand; as she walked, drawing more than one glance and comment to her pale face and strange manner; but she heeded nothing, only went on—on—on through street after street, knowing and caring not whither.

And presently, as she walked, she felt a heavy splash of rain upon her cheek, followed by another and then another, till at length the long-threatened storm was upon her. But still she hurried on. People in front, behind, and on all sides of her, ran like mad to every available shelter; but she looked quietly after them, still going on—on, while the drenching rain beat down upon her. She never heeded how it began to penetrate her shawl, to drench her hat and stream down her face. Suddenly, as she was in the act of crossing a street, hurrying to get out of the way of two cabs advancing in opposite directions, a glare of light flashed over the sky, followed by a loud peal of thunder.

The girl started, and came to a standstill in the middle of the road. The two cabmen, whose horses had shied violently, called to her to get out of the way, but she was dazzled and blinded,

and could not pay any heed to the directions.
Another moment and the two vehicles had dashed
by; as they did so she fell to the ground with a
cry of pain. The wheel of one of them had
knocked against her, sending a sharp pain up her
back, recalling the old days of agony. One or
two people who were passing came to her aid, but
almost without their help she staggered to her
feet and set off again on her journey.

This time, almost without knowing it, she turned
in a homeward direction, and presently reached
Wicker's Row. The ladies in the parlour were
just stepping into a cab which was at the door,
and drew back in horror from the bedraggled
figure who brushed past them in the hall, wondering who she could be.

She climbed the stairs, each step slower and
slower, and reached her room unquestioned. She
went in and shut the door, and began, in a me-
chanical sort of way, to take off her wrapper and
dress, now heavy with the rain, and clinging to
her, but she was so cold she did not feel them.

She was like a child who knew she had done
something foolish, and wished to hide the act. A
few minutes later she had hidden in a corner the
wet clothes, and donned the little black dress of
old. This done, she sat down in her chair, and
looked round her like one in a dream.

It was thus Sarah found her when, half an hour
later, she looked in for one of her stolen chats. It
was too dark—for the storm had not quite passed
over, and the dusk was coming on quickly—for

the girl to see her face plainly, but the sound of her voice, when she gave some random answer to her questions, struck Sarah as being unlike what it had been but a short time before.

At first she paid no heed to this for a little, thinking the storm had upset her nerves a little, but presently, as she went on talking, Lizette shivered violently.

" Why, what's up with you? " asked Sarah, breaking off in her sentence, and peering through the gloom at her.

" It's nothing," said Lizette, trying to control herself, but she seemed to have a fit of shivering, and her teeth began to chatter violently, and at length she was obliged to own to Sarah that both her head and back ached not a little.

The girl made her lie down, while she went and fetched what was to her a remedy for all ills—a cup of tea. But this did not seem to take any good effect. Lizette still seemed languid and drooping, shivering violently from time to time.

" I tell you what it is, Miss Lizet, you've got a cold, that's what you've got, and the best thing you can do is to go to bed this very minute."

Lizette resisted this command at first, but as the girl would not be denied, allowed her to help her to undress.

Once her head on the pillow, she seemed inclined to sleep.

" I'll look in again by-and-by," said Sarah, inwardly expressing herself rather strongly against the storm, the effect of which had been so disastrous, " and if anyone comes, I'll say you can't see 'em."

" Very well," said Lizette, turning away her face.

. . . .

A little later, Jerry came at last ; but oh, if he had only been a little sooner.

CHAPTER VIII.

SLANDEROUS TONGUES.

AND why did not Jerry come sooner? Why did
he stay away at all, and invent such a pack of lies?

I may as well explain the meaning of the mas-
querade at once. We know the task which our
hero had voluntarily taken upon himself,—the mis-
understanding which he had not attempted to
contradict, which had made the task easier, by
allowing him to pass for the sick girl's brother.
Otherwise, how could a friendship such as theirs
have prospered? Jerry was no fool in his dealings with those around him. He had not knocked
about the world for so long without learning
pretty nearly all there was to learn of its down-
ward paths. He knew only too well how many
grains of evil go to one ounce of good. He was
not given to be hard upon his fellow-men, but he
valued them by a standard which time and experience had raised; and being strictly just, did
not for a moment expect that they would rate
him any higher than themselves. Why should

he be thought any better than the rest of his fellow-men? Were not his life, birth, bringing-up, and daily association such as rather to discredit the idea, than otherwise?

It would seem, then, that if he feared what tongues might say, he should have passed by on the other side of the way, rather than have had anything to do with the sick girl,—have left her as he had found her, alone and cheerless, because the world—meaning those around her and him—might imagine mischief. This was the view of the matter which had appeared to Jerry when he first realised the desolation which he had lighted upon. Here was this girl, she whom he would have given so much to serve, in ever so small a way, a stranger and helpless in this big city, without a friend near her, or anyone to put out a hand to save her from the dreariness which was gradually drawing round her; and he—because the world said, " Nay "—must, if he cared for what might be thought and said by those who judged their neighbours by themselves, go on his way, leaving her alone and friendless as he had found her.

Jerry, we know, was but one of the rough-and-ready sort; but there were many who, with his sort of self-pride, would have shrank from treading the narrow path which lay before him. They might have feared for themselves, and for the fair young life thus voluntarily taken under their charge, and rather than run the risk of such a charge, had turned coward and fled from it. But Jerry was not one of these. He was not one to shrink from the task. His honesty and bravery would not let him, even if his love for this poor girl would have made it possible.

He did not look into his mind, but into his heart for guidance in the matter, and once his decision taken, he was as fearless and bold in the cause he had undertaken as any knight of old, though he did not don his lady's colours, and prepare to do battle with his good broadsword with any who dared so much as breathe a word against her.

People talk a lot about the good old days of chivalry. I, for one, believe as dauntless a spirit and as fearless a heart can beat beneath a rough, even ragged jacket, as beneath some coat of glittering mail.

Be this as it may, Jerry quietly, without any outward show, took upon himself the championship of the poor little seamstress, and for her sake fought a harder battle over self than is the lot of every soldier in this working life. He was going to fight for her against the world which had treated her so hardly, and that meant his having to use far more dangerous weapons than swords or daggers, without any shield save his knowledge and trust in himself, without hope of any reward save the satisfying of the great love in his heart, which would never, never die.

At first the struggle, in spite of the slowness of Lizette's recovery, was, comparatively speaking, an easy one. The evil he had most dreaded had, by a simple accident, been for a time averted—now, by an equally simple one, it threatened with

double force. There was what people would call
a deception, which would lend colour to any
report which might be circulated. One tiny pin-
hole of sunshine makes the gaslight sickly and pale.

We know how any underhand or double-dealing
was contrary to Jerry's nature, especially in the
present case. Falsehood and Lizette were as the
poles asunder in his mind, and bitterly he blamed
himself now for the false step which had caused
him to find shelter beneath the relationship which
had originated solely in Sarah's muddled brain.
I mean, of course, the mistake which made the
friends " brother and sister." The idea had been
purely a mistake : neither of those concerned had
set the ball rolling. What Jerry blamed himself
for was in not checking its course, since now
it threatened to fall upon not only him but his
sister, with double heaviness.

In what way, my reader may ask ? The accident which had disclosed the very innocent deception was this. The happy drive on Lizette's
birthday had brought it about. It had happened,
not by any peculiar chance, but rather, as might
have been naturally expected, that the little
chaise, with its burden of happiness, in one of
the busiest of streets, had overtaken and passed
a foot-passenger who had, on catching sight of
its occupants, expressed some interest. This was
none other than George Epsom.

He recognised Madame Petite and Jerry at
once, but was somewhat at a loss to know who
the third person could be.

" The old woman driving out in state like that!
She never told me she had any friends in the
place! Hey, what does she mean by playing fast
and loose with me? Friends! I didn't believe
she'd got one in the world, and doesn't want them.
Who the devil then is she with now, I wonder.
—— me, if I won't make it my business to find out."

Here followed a train of thought, in which the
little Frenchwoman was prime object; but presently Jerry came in for his share.

"—— him," muttered the jockey, lounging
alone in his usual dilatory way. " What's she
up to to have anything to do with him. I hate
that fellow. Sets himself up for being better than
any one else, and I'd swear he's as black as the
rest, only he knows how to keep it dark. I'd give
my life to catch him tripping. I always thought
there was something up between him and that
little German girl that Hermann let in so beauti-
fully. I wonder how Miss Rosa is behaving. If
all they say of her is true, he'd better have had
little meek face. At any rate, he entirely spoilt
Jerry's hash for him, for I'd lay a fiver he was
fool enough to be spoons on the girl. She was
pretty and bright enough, cuss her. Put Petite's
nose out of joint with the guv'nor, and if I'd have
been Hermann, I'd have done just the same. I
wonder how she got on after that smash up. By
Jove! it was a sickener. She must be quite done
for. At any rate, she won't be fit for the work
again, I should think."

A smile of satisfaction—cold and cruel—crossed

the jockey's face as he calculated upon the injury which the little fancy rider was likely to have sustained. Pity and sympathy had no place in his heart. He gave none and expected none— having no thought that the day might come when, strong and robust as he was now, might need both himself and find neither.

Health and strength were his now, and he fancied he could afford to strike his foot against she who had fallen.

He went on musing in this way for some little time, strolling down the sunny street along which the pleasure party had gone before him, till suddenly he came to a full stop, imbued with an idea.

This found vent in a string of oaths at his own stupidity in not discovering some fact before. Having thus relieved his feelings, he stood for a few moments knocking the pavement edge with his stick, apparently lost in thought. Presently he roused himself and strolled on again, taking this time note of the streets down which he passed, until he came to Wicker's Row. Here he paused again, repeating to himself the numbers of the houses, at length knocking at one and making some inquiries—not, it appeared, to any effect. This he did many times, till at length he reached Mrs Spicer's, where the reply made by Sarah to his question resulted in his stepping inside and interviewing "the missus," who, from his manner, it would appear, was not unknown to him.

At anyrate, the two engaged in a *tête-à-tête* of

some length, much to the curiosity of the "slavey," who, try as she would, could not overhear one word. She was not kept long in suspense. No sooner was her visitor gone than Mrs Spicer, by dint of pious ejaculations and half sentences of indignation, let out her secret.

Here was a pretty scandal!—a nice thing for a respectable lodging-house—enough to ruin the "lets" entirely. If only the parlours—two prim old maids—knew the truth, they would go straight out of the house at once! Their reason for remaining so long at the house was because its mistress had always been so particular. And here was a mare's nest right under their very noses—a scandal enough to ruin the character of any first-class boarding-house (which that in Wicker's Row certainly was not). What was to be done? Virtuous indignation suggested violent means—such as rooting out the evil at once; but this entailed a course which Mrs Spicer would rather not adopt.

She turned the matter over in her mind, and decided that the hushing-up process would be far the best for her pocket—if not for her conscience. So she determined to adopt it. But Mrs Spicer was a woman, and therefore possessed a tongue, which appendage had an unfortunate trick of running away with its owner. In this case it certainly did so. The result was that the jockey's few moments of mischief-making bore their fruit. If he had plotted for months to pay off the old score which he imagined he owed the little fancy rider, he could not have succeeded better.

Not brother and sister after all! Only a trumped-up tale to hide a relationship which would otherwise not have been accepted in a respectable lodging-house! Could anything be more disgraceful—scandalous? Just as if any respectable person would live under the roof with such a disreputable person as she, of whose existence they had hitherto been in ignorance.

This was what Mrs Spicer called hushing the matter up. The woman, I suppose, meant to hold her tongue, but found the task beyond her power. And so the secret leaked out. The story of a noble friendship, which, by the tainting breath of slander, was made to wear a cloak the colour of which was dark and sullen, the strings tied each day more tightly, until the knot seemed as if it would never be unfastened.

It was upon Jerry that the shadow first fell, and he was, in his unselfishness, glad it was so; for it was not so much the evil that he dreaded —a clear conscience need fear no accusation. His one thought was not for himself, but how the gloom might dim the sunshine which he could not but hope was beginning to beam in the life which he loved better than his own. He had known how it might be when he first took his task upon him; but now that the blow had fallen, if not unexpectedly, at least suddenly, and just when he was thinking he had not worked in vain,—come to dim the brightness, he knew not where next to turn his steps.

Only a few moments before he had met Madame Petite on the staircase, and learnt from her the news, which, in his exultation at the mischief he had effected, and partly out of the savage pleasure which he showed whenever he had a chance to torment her. The jockey had told her our hero had been as happy as he told himself he could hope to be now, which meant that the standard of content was far lower than it had been once upon a time.

When he had parted from Madame, he felt that he could not go and face Lizette after what he had heard ; he tramped along through the crowded streets, trying to solve the riddle in his mind— How was this matter to end ?

Of one thing he was assured. So long as it was possible, his little sister must be kept in ignorance that anything was amiss. Hitherto she had had no thought of evil, had trusted as implicitly as was deserved. Could he have the heart to go to her, and open her eyes to what she was too innocent and childlike to have guessed for herself?

No; at all risks, he must keep the knowledge from her as long as he could, trusting in fortune to favour him, as why should it not, since it had so often befriended the knights of old in their visible combats ? He was the poor child's brother ; he had taken the office long ago ; and he would keep it, in spite of all that slanderous tongues might say.

But this portion of the task was far more difficult than even he imagined. We none of us know how bitter is the struggle against the world's opinion which condemns us, until we are actually in the fight.

It is the work of Sisyphus—the mass is against us.

The very first visit that he had paid to Wicker's Row after the jockey had so kindly imparted his information on the subject to Mrs Spicer, was significant to him of what must follow.

The averted head of the shamefaced woman from the third floor seemed to tell him plainly that she would now no longer look on him as a friend, but rather as one whom even she might shun as one to be shunned, even by those who by experience have learnt to know evil from good; the ready greeting of the bold-looking man from the attics was even more suggestive. It was as if he hailed a fellow to the band to which he belonged. It was as well this view of the matter did not come to Jerry until he was fairly out of their reach, or I fear the torrent of passion which it roused within him might have been too much for his control.

It was perhaps as well, too, that he had not been brought in contact with the cause of so much mischief and unhappiness. The jockey, either by design or accident, did not cross his path.

There was danger in this subdued passion, this dogged patience. A good hand-to-hand tussle with the cause of his anger would have been a means of letting off the steam which might have saved much trouble and sorrow later on.

So the few days went by, and Jerry was no nearer having a plan than before he had tried his ruse—his pack of lies! On the day in which Lizette received the visit from Miss Jane Withers and her friend, he sat alone in his lodgings, wondering how on earth he was to find a way out of the difficulty.

A true statement of the case resolved itself into this—if his presence was to be the cause of evil to Lizette, he must go away,—leave her.

Go away! That meant to give up the one little ray of comfort there was left in his life,—to give up his usefulness to this poor girl,—his right of protectorship and guardianship,—the only way he had of showing her that there was some good in the world still. Leave her! That meant to leave her to fight the battle for herself, her part in which he would have so gladly borne,—to leave her alone and friendless as he had found her; nay, worse, for supposing she knew the reason of his desertion, might she not think it insufficient,— think him mean and cowardly?

And yet how could he stand by and let one breath of evil taint the purity he prized so highly?

The struggle was a long and bitter one. But self was defeated. Love — the honest, stedfast love of a brother for a sister,—a fragile child in the ways of the world—conquered.

Jerry made no vow—uttered no strong heroic expression expressive of his sentiments, but deep down in that poor bruised heart of his there was a steady set purpose to do what was right,—at all costs to himself to save Lizette from any chance of ill.

This conclusion arrived at, he did not wait for time to change his mind, but took his hat and set off to Wicker's Row.

He would pay his visit as if nothing had happened. However he would scrape up enough lies to describe his doings of the few days he did not know, and later on—say at the end of the week— announce his intention of throwing up his engagement at the Hall, to return to his old life. Perhaps in the roaming life of some travelling show things would seem easier. He would make whatever provision he could for Lizette's comfort,—see her safe in good hands, and then go away—not to lose sight of her, but to watch over her from the distance,—be her guardian angel, indeed. At the thought, as he walked slowly on his way towards Wicker's Row, he smiled a rather watery sort of a smile, which agreed only too well with the sleepless look on his face. This relaxation of countenance attracted the attention of a poor little flower-girl whose perishable goods were fast fading under the heat of the afternoon sun. She sprang up from the doorway where she had been resting for a moment in the shade, and solicited his custom. He looked down pityingly at her, then —did not fling a copper into her basket, or drop some seed of flattery into her mind, but laid his hand gently on her head, and spoke kindly to her.

"I don't want any flowers, thank you, little one," he said, "and I'm afraid no one else will, unless you freshen them up a bit. There's the tap near—what do you say? Let's see what we can do."

And he turned down a narrow alley which seemed to be unknown to her, and held the fading blossoms under the cool dripping water, then gave them back into their owner's charge. "They'll come up after a bit, if you don't keep 'em in the sun."

The child stared with big eyes at him, but unused to being so kindly and considerately noticed, forgot to be bold and saucy, as she had been taught.

"I never thought o' doing that. Maybe they'll go now. I've only took twopence all the morning. Here's one as ain't no use, it's gone too far. You can 'ave it if yer like. Roses is so cheap now, no one wants 'em," and she held out the withered blossom.

Jerry would have taken it—thinking, I think, of another flower which no one wanted—but ere he could clasp it, a great hulking fellow lounging by brushed against him, and knocking it from the child's fingers, crushed it beneath his foot.

There it lay in the dirt, it that had once been so fair, bruised and dead in the dust of the street.

The child bounded off after the man, and was soon pestering him to buy, he replying, first by words of coarse flattery—for the child was pretty in a rough, uncultivated sort of way—then by coarser oaths, for her to leave him alone.

Jerry turned away feeling sick at heart, thinking of the other rose which he had chosen, instead of something more precious. But he did not see in its story a different meaning to that of the flower on the pavement.

This little incident, however, had roused him from the reverie into which he had fallen, and he became aware of the signs in the sullen sky.

"There's a storm coming," he thought—taking off his hat and looking up into the sky,—"I'll hurry a bit; Lizette may not like to be alone when it breaks."

Then into his mind came that thought, how he must leave her to face the other storm, and his honest heart cursed the slandering tongues which had come between them—those evil-doers who see good in no one. At anyrate he would go to Lizette and cheer her during this weather's wrath. It might be the last time they would be together.

He turned on his way; but as he did so, the splash of the first rain-drop fell upon his hand. He started to run, but in another moment the full fury of the torrent was upon him, and breathless and panting he obeyed the impulse which bade him seek shelter in a shed near at hand.

At anyrate, he thought, "Lizette is safe from this; no doubt that big Sarah will go to her."

He did not guess that at that very moment Lizette was trudging through the rain, exposed to all the mercy of the storm, or he would have gone out from his shelter and never rested till he had found her.

As it was, he stood in the shed chatting with a baker's man who had sought the same protection, and did not notice how time was passing, till a chance remark made him aware of it.

"As late as that," he said, starting up; "why, I started nearly an hour and a half ago."

And although the storm was by no means over, he set out once more on his way, passing by a shop in which he saw the little flower-girl whom he had befriended, with an empty basket, but a face flushed and excited, as she tossed her head and looked up into the face of the big, hulking-looking man, who lounged over the counter beside her and held a glass towards her. Jerry did not see them, but hurried quickly on.

A few moments later he reached Wicker's Row. The door was opened to him by Sarah, who started violently on seeing him, as if he had been a ghost.

He began to say something lightly to her, but was stopped by a look on her face.

"Why, Sarah, what's the matter?" he asked. "Has 'the missus' being going it very much since I saw you last?"

As he spoke he attempted to pass her, but she barred the way.

"You can't go up," she said stolidly.

"Why not?" asked Jerry, turning suddenly on her, his heart full of sudden fear. "There's nothing wrong?"

" No," said Sarah ; " but Miss Lizette ain't very well. The storm's given her one of her old head-aches, and she says she won't see nobody to-night."

There was a meaning look on the usually stolid face as the girl spoke, which puzzled Jerry for a moment ; then he thought he understood.

So he said to himself, " It's got to her ears. They couldn't even be content with making me miserable, but they must have at her. And she won't see me again. Well, I suppose she's right, I'll go."

And without a word he turned away out into the street again. But his thoughts were very bitter as he walked home through the rain, and his tricks and jokes in the ring that night fell very flat—I suppose because his heart was not in them. He did not go to Wicker's Row that day or the day after, but the day after that he called, not with the intention of going in, but just to gain some news — the errand boy, and source of his former information, having been dismissed the day before, on a charge of stealing the top floor lodger's boots, afterwards found behind some rubbish on the landing (they were straightway converted by Mrs Spicer into capital, which she did not send to the discharged odd boy to defray the expenses of his loss of character. What the future of this ill-used youth was, I do not know, but if the tradition of a dog with a bad name was falsified in him, it was through no exertion on the part of his fellow-men).

For want of this means of communication, Jerry,

therefore, went in person to the Row, and was surprised and dismayed to find that Lizette was still unable to see him, being, in fact, far from well.

His ready fears were at once aroused. He subjected Sarah to a strict examination on the subject, and succeeded in eliciting from her information enough to thoroughly alarm him for the result of this sudden attack.

He did not say much : but there and then, in spite of the risk of being late at the Hall, whither he was bound, set off in search of Dr Woodward.

He luckily found the doctor at home, just in the middle of his tea. This meal, however, on hearing what little Jerry had to tell, he left unfinished, and went to pay his former little patient a visit.

What self - denying, hard - worked creatures doctors are. And yet, because their presence usually means trouble and sorrow, how many forget that it is not they who bring, but relieve it, and think lightly of services which cost so much mental exertion, to say nothing of the amount of actual labour which going from case to case requires, the awful amount of responsibility which rests upon them—a life loved and worshipped, or one of sin and unrepented evil, may be cast away by a moment's carelessness or forgetfulness—the never-resting toil which leaves no moment of the day to be called free—no hour in which the weapons of defence and watching may be laid aside, for at any moment the battle of life and death may have to be renewed.

Jerry went with Dr Woodward to the door of

No. 19, the Row, then stayed walking up and down outside till he should come out. The time —as when does it not, when we are waiting— seemed like hours. In reality it was only a few moments. At length, when it seemed to Jerry that he could bear the suspense no longer, the door opened and the doctor came out.

Jerry bounded to meet him.

" Well ? " he asked eagerly.

The doctor looked rather perplexed than grave. He did not answer for a few moments, then looked up suddenly with those keen grey eyes of his from under his bushy brows, and asked gruffly, almost angrily,—

" Are you her brother, or not ? "

" I am not," replied Jerry.

" I am her friend—at least I want to be."

As he spoke he returned the doctor's gaze with one the frankness of which was almost defiance. The doctor had just heard that tale, which had made him look less kindly on his little patient, and he was prepared to make it his duty to stop the mischief which he suspected was the cause of the attack of Lizette's. He meant to have spoken his mind very freely to Jerry, but there was something in this look which met his, that disarmed him.

He did not pretend to be a very advanced student in the study of character, but if ever a face disarmed suspicion and distrust, it was the young clown's at that moment.

We know it was far from being a handsome one—and no change had come over it in that respect—but the resolute, open-hearted expression in the grey-green eyes—the firm set of the big mouth—the half-sad, half-defiant look on the irregular features, made their common-placeness be forgotten.

"Want to be her friend, do you?" said the doctor, going to make certain sure. "And do you suppose you will do it by bringing shame and disgrace on her?"

He used hard words; but he knew of old that to probe a wound one must use sharp instruments. And he acted rightly.

Jerry winced perceptibly under the blow—it was so direct. The colour rushed to his cheeks—he took a step forward, and raised his clenched fist. But it did not fall. The doctor did not move, only stood looking searchingly with his bright, far-seeing eyes.

This time Jerry could not return the glance. A mist was before him. The colour fled from his face as quickly as it had come—his lip quivered—his hand fell open to his side, and he turned away.

The doctor made a movement forward.

"Where are you going?" he asked.

"Away from here," said Jerry, very quietly. "If my being here'll do her harm, I'll go away."

"Then you don't love her?" There was a trace of questioning in the doctor's tone, but all the same it was kind, almost gentle.

It was too much for Jerry. He gave way. Turning quickly, he confronted his questioner like a lion at bay.

"Don't love her," he said, in a hoarse whisper.

"Don't love her! I love her better than I've ever loved a soul else. Don't love her! Why, if it'd bring back to her what she's lost, wouldn't I go straight to hell this very moment. Ay, that I would, if only it'd undo what's done."

The expression on his lips sounded profane and melodramatic, but the tone spoke more truly than the words. Dr Woodward was convinced. He laid his hand in a fatherly way upon the speaker's shoulder.

"Perhaps there's an easier way to put things right than that, lad. I believe you are honest. If I doubted, it was because one sees so much evil one hardly recognises the good — but I believe you're true."

At this Jerry's reserve gave way entirely, and standing in the busy street, as man to man will speak, he told the story of his love, which had never yet entered any ears but those of poor Smith, now far away, lost in the mazes of this big, busy world.

The doctor listened quietly and sympathised, though he said but little. Presently he drew a note-book from his pocket, tore out a page, handed it to Jerry with a pencil, seemingly bidding him write something. Jerry, however, said he was no scholar, so the doctor scribbled a few lines himself, signing Jerry's name at the end.

This note Jerry carried to No. 19, and gave to Sarah, with the injunction to carry it to Lizette.

A little later the two men parted—the one to hurry off to some other battlefield of pain and suffering, to fight over again the weary struggle, which, even if he gains, will be but giving strength for a future defeat, which, no matter how often the former conquests, must come at last—the other to go amidst fun and jollity, to take his place in the ring, to joke and gambol like an empty-headed brainless fool, while his limbs seemed too heavy even to support him, and his heart was heavy with the old aching pain.

But his audience knew nothing of this. They saw only the quaintly-dressed figure, the painted face. They had come to laugh, to be amused, to be merry. If this jester was dull, his jokes flat, let him stand aside and make room for a bigger fool. This often happens in our lives as well as in the ring.

The performance over, instead of lingering as he sometimes did for a chat with some of his fellow-artists, or to watch with professional interest the performance, Jerry hurried off home.

On his way he went into a stationer's shop and bought a quire of cream-laid paper—the best to be got—don't laugh at him, dear reader—a bottle of ink, and a pennyworth of nibs.

Reaching his lodgings he sat down at the table and prepared, as might have been expected, to write a letter. He did this very leisurely, and yet he must have been inwardly excited or very absent-minded, for he entirely forgot to take off his hat.

It would appear to any one watching him that this letter was going to cost him some trouble. At starting he broke the neck of the ink bottle—I should say the chimney of the little cottage in which was contained the black fluid so called—some of which he managed to spill over the table-cloth—one of those many-coloured ones which seem peculiar to lodging-houses—tried and discarded each of the four nibs in turn, and at length, selecting one at random, started on the paper.

This operation was, he found, far easier than it looked, he not being much of a scholar, as he said, but I do not think it was his want of learning which stood in the way, but the state of his mind, which might truly be described as chaotic. He was in the enviable condition of having a letter to write and not knowing what to say—or rather of having something to say and not knowing how to express it.

Added, therefore, to his pen shying violently, as he expressed it, almost every moment at some capital or extra long words, which it seemed to look upon in the light of hedges and ditches, he made so many false starts, each time taking a fresh field, *i.e.*, sheet of paper. Once he heaved a sigh, ran his fingers through his short hair, and discovered his hat.

He took it off, and, looking absently at it, laid it aside, took a fresh sheet of paper, stared at it blankly for several moments as if he expected the words in his mind by some unknown process to imprint themselves upon the page, roused himself, made a dash with the pen at the ink—dipping it "up to the hilt"—then held it suspended in the air, while he bit his nails thoughtfully. Presently he was roused again by finding himself digging the nib into the table—an action which did not tend to improve it—and again set to work. It was truly comical to see him bending in a rick neck attitude over the table, grasping the pen resolutely in his big clumsy fingers—by this time plentifully besmeared with ink—his face going into all sorts of grimaces in his attempts to fulfil a task which in these enlightened days would have been nothing to a child of one quarter his age. Such were the fruits of being born before the School Board had come into power.

Jerry's attempts at penmanship were anything but successful. He had no idea the task would have proved one of such difficulty, but he struggled manfully on, by-and-by untying his necktie—which, of course, was indicating its wearer's mind by being most obsteperous—and laying it aside. After this he seemed to get on a little better—actually wrote three consecutive lines on one page, of which achievement he was so proud, that in flourishing his pen over it he succeeded in ornamenting the whole with half a dozen big blots, which he tried in vain to remove with his handkerchief—not, I am bound to say, with any beneficial results.

This failure upset him not a little. He got up, stretched his legs, which were stiff with the cramped position in which he had been sitting.

Had he been in a more jovial frame of mind he would have tried what a somersault would do to "ease the joints." As it was, he walked quickly up and down the room several times, causing dear Miss Jane, who, as usual, was lingering in the passage, a severe heartache least he should be ill, and at last, moved by a sudden impulse, flung off his coat, plunged his head into a basin of cold water till every hair of his head stood up like a bristle with a dew-drop at the end of it, and after shaking himself like a dog, sat down once more at the table.

By this time his numerous false starts, shying, and backing, had made such a hole in his quire of paper, that if he did not "go a-head" a bit this time, it would be necessary for him to lay in a fresh stock of materials. But it was now so late that most of the shops would be closing, if not closed, so that if he wanted to write his letter at all, it must be on the one remaining sheet. . This perhaps accounted for his preparation.

He looked ruefully at the torn and crumpled scraps with which by this time the table and floor were littered, then drew the unused piece towards him, and without giving himself time to think, wrote whatever came first into his mind—which meant the red-hot phrases which came straight from his heart. It is a queer picture he presents.

His legs have twisted themselves round the table leg in a way that gives one the cramp to see, so uncomfortable it looks—at his best he never was graceful, as we know ; his back is bent in another awkward cramp-producing position ; his head is bent so low that the bone stud in his sadly-crumpled shirt-front is leaving a big dent in his chin ; the water from his hair is trickling down his neck ; his shirt is open at the neck, showing his brown throat ; his sleeves rolled up to his elbows, displaying a pair of muscular brown arms ; his eyes are wide open, staring down at the page, his eyebrows almost meeting over them in wrinkles which pucker his low forehead ; his cheeks are now puffed out, now drawn in ; his mouth seems doing its best to cover the whole of his face by its distortions, but his stumpy inky fingers resolutely grapple the pen as in a vice, and the words are fast flowing from beneath it.

And what is this important document upon which he is so busily engaged?

It is intended for no eye but that of her to whom it is addressed, but we may look over his shoulder without his knowing. What we read is this. I correct the spelling, which was not of the best.

" My " (scratched out) " DEAR LIZ,—Don't think me bold-like in writing you a line. I hadn't meant to, only I've got something particular to say to you —leastways, something as I wants to say, which I hope you won't take amiss, knowing as you do how pleased I'd have been to say what I've got to say if I could have seen you for a bit, which, as I can't, I must write, though how I'll get it on to paper I don't know, seeing I ain't, as

you know, anything of a scholar. Well, I saw
the doctor to-night, and he told me about your
wanting to go into the hospital, which, I says with
him, would be best, perhaps. They'll bring you
round sooner there than anywhere. Don't you remember how they pulled Will Breakneck through
when he broke his collar bone in the thirty feet
fall, and— But this ain't what I wants to say.
What it is, is this—don't read any more if you
haven't a mind—but I want to ask you if you've
ever thought you'd like to marry me, leastways,
if you'd like for us to be married now? I have
thought of it before, but I know I ain't the
sort of fellow a girl like you'd care for. But
you're ill now, and I thought it'd cheer you a bit
if you had a friend you could count on. I thought
we'd get along—brother and sister, like, as you
said—but you know now folks won't let us. It'd
be different if you'd let me be someone nearer. Be
my wife—marry me—I don't ask nothing more; I
daresay you'll wonder why I ask at all. It's because
you seem so sad and lonesome; you're ill makes
you so, but I'm your only friend, and I want to
help you, if only you'll let me. Marry me, and
I'll work for you till I drop: we'll share together.
I can earn enough for two. Will you let me?
Will you trust me to do as I say? I only ask to
marry you. I won't say a word about love. I
know yours is given, and if it wasn't, I'm not the
sort of fellow you'd choose. I only want to help
you,—to be your friend better than I am now.
When you are my wife, they won't dare to say

what they do now. What's the use of denying
what they say. They wouldn't believe it. Why
should they? It isn't likely they'll think me
better than other chaps. I know I'm only an ill-
bred fellow, come from nobody knows where.
a-going nobody cares. Why should they? You
know what our life is? It don't make us exactly
gentlemen. I ain't got none to speak up for me.
I never set up for being better than I am, so how
are they to know I don't mean no harm by you.
It ain't for myself that I minds particular what
they say. They might have known it was lies
to speak of you as they do—lies, wicked, cruel
lies, every word. I ain't good at speechifying,
but I do say this,—I hope I may die straight off
in the ring with the war-paint on, and that they'll
bury me in it, if ever I give them reason to tell
anything but lies of you. If you'd let me be your
husband, they'd have to hold their tongues. Will
you think over it a bit? Don't hurry, and don't
think I'll think badly of you if you can't say 'Yes.'
—Your obedient servant,   JERRY BOLTON.

" *P.S.*—Please excuse the blots and bad writing. If it is ' No'—the answer—don't say anything, we'll drop the subject."

That was all.

A queerly-worded epistle, in very shaky writing,
with a pretty liberal sprinkling of blots and much
scratching out and correction where the pen had
run away with the writer's ideas, and he had

had to pull up short. And yet, as one read it, one forgot the sorry performance it was,—forgot the queer figure the writer cut—his strange costume—his plain looks—and remembered only the brave heart which was thus laid bare to the core.

"I don't ask for love, for I know yours is given."

The sentence was a little tragic in tone, but it was the key to a riddle of a life which few could have given so readily. Jerry, Jerry—as you lay aside your pen at last, and say your task is done, you little know that this bit of work would shame many a deed which is recorded on a roll of honour.

A few moments later Mrs Spicer answered a ring at the bell of No. 19 Wicker's Row. It was dark, and she could only see a coatless figure, who handed her a letter, saying,—

"Be sure and give that to Miss Hartzmann," and straightway vanished.

The landlady turned the letter over and over, eyeing it with a curiosity peculiar to landladies. It was too late for her to take it up—indeed it was only by chance that it could have been delivered at the house, Mrs Spicer being engaged in taking a last prowl round her premises before retiring to rest.

She therefore laid the note on the hatstand, where it would be sure to catch Sarah's eye the first thing in the morning. This done, she retired to rest—of which, I fear, there was but little for two persons connected with the writing and sending of that same unpretending-looking note.

CHAPTER IX.

"GO AWAY."

IT was the next day, about seven o'clock in the
evening, when Jerry at last went to pay his
promised visit. It may seem strange that, knowing what he did, he did not do so earlier; but
although, as a rule, the worst is less hard to bear
than suspense, in this case Jerry did not find
it so.

All the morning he had been restless and un-
easy—full of all sorts of doubts and fears concerning his last night's work. At one time he
wished it undone—called himself a fool and all
sorts of bad names for trying to force his attentions where he knew they were not welcome, if,
after all, needed; at another, he persuaded himself that he was right—that he he had acted for
the best, and Lizette would know that. Then
again he recalled, word for word, what he had
said in the letter—first terribly afraid that it
might be misunderstood—that he had not said
enough—that he had said too much; then trying

to reassure himself that it was what he meant, and if any harm were done, he would explain and correct all when he saw Lizette ; and then again remembering how poor a scholar he had shown himself—sorely afraid lest he, a great big clumsy ill-bred fellow that he was, had been too presumptuous.

With such doubts and fears he tormented himself all day, until at length, as no word or sign (as he had dared to hope might) had come from Lizette, he could control himself and his fears no longer. He would go and see her for the last time—beg her forgiveness for having worried her with his silly fancy, and say good-bye—for Dr Woodward had named the following day for that of her removal to the hospital.

Accordingly, as I have said, seven o'clock on that Sunday evening saw our hero once more seeking admittance at No. 19 the Row.

Sarah opened the door to him, and giving him no time to ask questions, told him, Miss Lizet was about the same, but he could go up ; she was expecting him.

Expecting him! How those words sent Jerry's heart thumping against his side, till it seemed, as he made his way upstairs, that he heard the sound of three steps instead of two.

The tumult of feelings in his mind, the hopes and fears, now all mixed up together, can better be imagined than described.

What if, after all, his letter had accomplished its purpose? What if Lizette were not angry—

what if—and at the thought his heart beat louder
still, till he thought it would burst—what if
Lizette had been waiting all day to give her
answer? What if she were waiting even now to
put the trust in him for which he had begged,
waiting to say that little word "yes," which
meant so much to him?

With a sudden bound he sprang up the remaining stairs, and reached the third landing. Here,
without noticing the sad-faced woman, who passed
him looking sadder and more weary than ever, he
knocked softly at the front room door.

A low "Come in" told him that his visit was
indeed expected, and turning the handle with a
hand that trembled slightly, so great had grown
his excitement during those past few moments,
he entered, then paused to let his eyes get accustomed to the uncertain light, for the days were
beginning to draw in, and it was already getting
dusk.

After a moment, he saw Lizette lying on the
couch by the window, her face turned to greet
him, white and pain-drawn, reminding him forcibly
of the day when he had first found her. And now
was he come to claim her entirely, or to lose her
for ever? The question was not to be answered
immediately.

Lizette might have been expecting him, but as
to the waiting, that was quite another thing.

Jerry waited for her to speak, I think, because
he was afraid that if he opened his mouth his
tongue would run away with his thoughts.

Lizette's greeting might guide him a little as to what he was to do.

She raised herself slightly, and held out her hand with a wan, feeble attempt at a smile.

" It is very good of you to come to see me," she said, with just a touch of sadness in her tone, to make it doubly sweet, at least to Jerry's ear.

" No it isn't," he said deprecatingly. " I came because I thought you'd like me to, that's all. At least," thinking this not exactly the right way of putting it, " I came because—well," in despair to find a better reason, " I came because I wanted to."

" All the same, it is good of you," repeated Lizette, as if she felt she must say something. There was a silence, to break which she said, " Won't you sit down ? " an invitation not usually necessary.

" No, thanks. I ain't going to stay long," said Jerry, adding, thinking he saw a look of relief on her face, " I only ran in for a moment to see "—he pulled up short, having nearly said what he did not mean to—" to see how you are." And he went a step nearer.

He forgot Sarah had already supplied his information.

" I'm pretty well to-night, thank you—at least as well as I shall be, Dr Woodward says, until they see what they can do for me at the hospital. But I'm afraid it won't be any use. I shall never be any use in the world."

She spoke with such a return of her old desponding manner, that the hope which burnt in her listener's heart began to lose some of its brightness.

"Don't you fret," he blundered out. "They're mighty clever at these hospitals; they've pulled folks round as is been farther gone than you have. Look at Will Breakneck. How did you get bad all of a sudden again? I thought your back was getting quite strong."

As he looked towards Lizette for his answer, he saw a faint glow of colour rising to the pale face, which was suddenly turned away from him. He had touched on dangerous ground.

He had, he knew, mentioned Will Breakneck in the letter. He waited a moment, thinking Lizette might say something on the subject, but she did not, and to cover the pause, he made some trivial remark about the weather, and for the next few minutes they spoke about any but the subject which each had in mind.

Meanwhile, Lizette did not seem at her ease. She played nervously with a frill of her dress, and kept turning her face away, as if she did not care to meet his glance.

And Jerry? Noting these signs with a quickness which was born of his mixed feelings, his heart, poor fellow, was slowly sinking down into his boots. He stood leaning against the table, twirling his hat in his hands, and every moment feeling as if he must out with the question which was on his tongue.

The time flew by in this fruitless chat, and still

Lizette made no sign, said no word to revive the fast-dying hope.

Silence meant the refusal of his proposal—so Jerry had willed it. But he had already began to think that a " no," no matter how uttered—even contemptuously or angrily — would have been better than this.

He could see, even while she tried to speak calmly and quietly, that Lizette was excited and seemed to be holding herself in control. What should he do? While trying to answer this question—which of course took no little time—he wandered off into any amount of chit-chat, asking questions the answers to which he did not listen to, gave replies he did not intend, got confused, broke off suddenly in the midst of a long, dry tale he had drifted into, and relapsed into silence. Lizette in vain tried to rouse him. He seemed suddenly to have become dumb. He resisted her attempts with what seemed to her coldness, and even annoyance, until at last she too, with a heavy sigh, became silent.

For some time Jerry sat staring stolidly at the shabby carpet at his feet, nursing his hat on his knees, for by this time he had sat down on the edge of a chair in a most uncomfortable position, longing to say what was in his mind,—to make this uncertainty sure. The suspense was terrible. The poor little flickering hope was fast dying away, smouldering into grey dull ashes.

Presently he felt he could stand it no longer. He must either speak or go. He would do no

good by hanging on by a straw. The good-bye
must come. The sooner it was over the better.
He rose suddenly—so suddenly indeed that Lizette
started, and the ready colour flooded her face.

This attack had evidently affected her nerves.

"It's getting late," said Jerry, rubbing his hat
vigorously with his sleeve, for the sake of venting
his feelings in some action, "and I think I'll be
going on home."

It was only a quarter past seven; but I suppose
he wished to make up for his want of rest on the
night before.

A pause. Lizette did not press him to stay, or
attempt to say good-bye.

"There's nothing I can do for you?"

"Nothing, thank you," was the quiet reply—
recalling that scene in the stables so many days
ago, when he had asked her those unnecessary
questions, and she had answered just like this;
only now she seemed trying to battle against the
hopelessness,—to speak almost indifferently. The
words brought back that night vividly to his mind,
and he felt the hope grow fainter and fainter, till
there was nothing but a tiny spark left; for keeping
which alive he blamed himself severely.

"Then I'll say good-bye," he said, holding out
his hand; "and mind, I'll always be your friend,
whatever happens. I'm a rough sort of chap, but
I'll be ready at any time if you want help."

Lizette again said "Thank you" very quietly;
but the thin, hot little hand which lay so passively
within Jerry's strong one trembled suspiciously.

He had been holding it loosely, as if afraid to crush it, but now his clasp suddenly tightened. He would not go without a word. Suppose there had been some mistake—letters often get mislaid. Suppose this one had never reached her—suppose, after all— Up flared the hope again. And Jerry asked abruptly,—" You got my letter ? "

" Yes." As he spoke, he looked down into the brown eyes which drooped suddenly under his gaze, and again Lizette turned her head away as she answered " Yes."

Jerry waited, but silence followed the one word ; and he knew he had had his answer ; he knew that, though it pained Lizette to give it, for in his earnestness he had kept possession of her hand ; and though she tried to turn away he could see that strange determined look on her face, which made it impossible to doubt her intention.

Jerry stood for a moment looking down at her in her helplessness, with a fierce, longing, hopeless look in his eyes. He felt somehow as if he could not take this answer. Why was he not allowed to give the help which was so much needed ? Why must he go away when some one he loved was so lonely and friendless ?

If she had only been as gay and well as she had been a short week ago, he might have felt it less hard, but now that she was ill and in trouble, he felt he must make one effort.

He would tell her to forget all about the letter, to come away with him somewhere, where the tales would not be known, where they would begin life again as brother and sister, let those think of harm who might. He would defy them; he would—

The words of passionate entreaty were almost on his lips, but a glance at the white wan face stayed him.

The thought of any breath of evil against Lizette seemed to hold him back. The choice was a hard one. Lizette decided it for him. Looking up—perhaps wondering at his silence—finding her eyes fixed upon his with that strange look in them, she withdrew her hand suddenly from his and said hurriedly,—

"Did you not say to me it was time for you to go? Do not let me to keep you. Good-bye; and thank you for being so very kind for me."

Her voice faltered a little, and Jerry said gruffly, because of that lump which would rise to his throat,—

"Don't thank me, there ain't no cause, and don't worry yourself. You'll be all right after a bit. Don't think anything more about me, as we can't go on as we have. Don't be angry for my thinking about the marrying. I didn't think you'd mind. I'm sorry what's done can't be undone. You aren't angry with me—are you?"

Poor Lizette! Her face was hidden in her hands now, lest he should see the flush of shame which flooded it.

Angry with him for thinking of marrying! This was the last drop of bitterness.

Lizette's bosom heaved convulsively—she was fast losing all self-control.

"I didn't mean to hurt you," said Jerry, his voice also beginning to shake. "Don't fret, Liz, it'll all come right by-and-by when this has blown over."

Lizette once more held out her hand.

"Good-bye," she said, and he knew she wished him to go. "Good-bye—for ever!"

"Good-bye, but don't say for ever, Liz. We'll be friends at least. No one can say a word agin that. We'll meet again some day. I'll always like to know how you're getting on. You know I can't help this."

"No, no!" said Lizette, with a sort of despairing cry. "I know all of what you would say. Go now. Please go quickly."

The look of pain on her face was unmistakable. She had raised herself to a sitting position, and held out both her hands, as if to push him away.

She did not mean to be unkind, and Jerry did not think her so, but his heart was very bitter as he turned to obey her.

"Good-bye," he said quietly once more.

But something in his face must have touched Lizette, for she sprang to her feet.

"Jerry!"

He turned and went slowly to where she stood holding out both her hands for him to take, with that pretty foreign gesture off which cold English manners had not yet broken her.

"Don't think me to be ungrateful. I want to

hope you may be happy when you marry your wife.
I do hope it indeed. Good-bye—my brother."

This was the last straw. Jerry did not say a
word. The next moment he was gone.

The girl, standing alone in the darkened room,
listened till the sound of his footsteps had died
away on the stair, watched his figure, as slowly,
like one returning from a long weary journey,
he passed down the street, and was lost in the
distance.

Then at last she realised that she was truly
alone, and forgetting the lesson she had tried to
teach herself in the dark hours of the night,—
the shame which she felt because of the secret in
her heart—forgetting all else save that the good-
bye so lately spoken might—nay, it almost seemed
must be—for ever, she flung herself face downwards on the couch, and wept the first tears of
womanhood—far, far more bitter than those of
childhood, whose mind is scarcely yet its own.

.   .   .   .

On the morrow, the parlour ladies, on their return from their morning constitutional, found a
cab waiting at the door of No. 19—a rare occurrence when they were not at home.

The mystery was explained. As they passed
up the stairs they met Dr Woodward coming
down, half supporting, half carrying a slight
figure, whose white pain-drawn face, with the
scar on one side, looked strangely pitiful.

"Who can she be?" whispered Miss Mary, the
younger of the two maidens.

"Hush!" frowned her elder sister, marching straight on with an erect head, like a war-horse scenting powder. "It's that girl Mrs Spicer spoke of. I see she is going. I told the landlady if she did not, we should."

"Oh," said Miss Mary, preparing to imitate her sister, but adding, with a second glance at the white face below, "but she does look ill, poor thing. And so young to be so wicked. And yet Dr Woodward seems to treat her kindly, and Sarah tells me—"

"Doctors have to do their duty among all sorts of people, and I wish, Mary, you would not listen to so many of Sarah's tales. She is a low-bred, ignorant servant, and this girl is not at all deserving of your pity."

"Don't you think some one ought to tell her how wrong she is," replied Miss Mary. "Suppose I were to."

"Mary, what next? You seem to forget you are a member of the Female Mission."

It was Miss Henrietta who forgot this, but Miss Mary was awed, as she always was by the fact recalled to her mind, and meekly followed her sister, thus losing a chance of doing a good action.

By this time Lizette was being lifted by the doctor into the cab, for he had found her so weak that morning that he had decided to see her himself safely to the hospital, which was some distance from the town. It was only one of the many kind actions which will be put down to this good, if rough, man's account.

And so Lizette was going from the place which had been her home for so long. She could never have imagined how dear that poor little room on the third floor had come to be to her, until she came to leave it. She forgot that it is memories, not walls, which make a place " home."

It seemed to her when she passed the threshold for the last time, that she was cutting away the last link between herself and every friend she had in the world. If only there had been some one there to wish her God-speed,—to speak of the time when she should be out in the world again— if ever that should be—things would not have seemed so dreary.

Even Sarah had not come to say good-bye. No doubt this was Mrs Spicer's doings: she never forgave the girl for her staunch defence of Lizette; but, all the same, it was hard to go without a word from anybody. It was harder still when in the hall, to see those two old young maids stare fixedly at her, whisper perhaps some comments upon her scarred face, and then turn their heads away, as if the sight of it was painful to them.

How much would a word of pity have been worth to the poor, starving heart. But a member of the Female Mission has her character to look after; far more precious a duty than comforting a stray, and to them lost, sheep.

But some one else who, as she had been taken into her mistress's service without any recommendation, and, furthermore, belonged to no

Mission or Friendly Society, did the duty that her betters had left undone.

Just as Dr Woodward closed the cab door, with an injunction to the driver to drive as fast as he could, as the journey would rob him (the doctor) of far more time than he could conveniently spare, a big figure came flying from the house. It was Sarah, looking more "slavish" than ever, in a dirty cotton dress, tucked up to show a ragged petticoat, a dirtier apron, a begrimed pair of arms and face, and a duster over her head, beneath which short, greasy locks of hair were indiscriminately looped up by sundry very leaden-looking hairpins.

How she had managed to escape from the supervision of Mrs Spicer's eagle eye was unknown, but there she was, clattering down the steps, in her haste almost leaving behind one of her down-at-the-heel boots, the elastic of which was only called so by courtesy.

" Stop a bit, cabby," she cried, hailing that worthy with scant ceremony. " I ain't a-going to let Miss Lizet go without saying good-bye."

With this she introduced her big shoulders and head into the cab, nearly crushing the window frame, and causing Dr Woodward's hat to fall into the bottom of the vehicle.

" I couldn't get away a minute sooner, or I'd have come like a shot. Missus has been that rampageous this morning. She's set her heart on doing a six weeks' wash, though we only had one last Tuesday" (the logic of this statement was hardly apparent), "and there won't be no peace

for the wicked till it's done. I left her taking water
out of the copper, that's been agone and bust itself
somewhere, and is a-flooding the scullery. A nice
mess : it'll take goodness knows how long to clean
up ; but there, I knew as she couldn't leave off, so
I run up to see yer. I'm awful sorry you're going,
but when you comes out of the hospital, you'll let
me know, won't you ? "

It was plain, by the way she was running on,
that the girl was trying to hide her emotion ; but
now she paused for breath, dived into her pocket,
and drew out a little flat pincushion made of two
pieces of cardboard, covered with silk (now very
faded and greasy) and sewn together. This she
thrust into Lizette's hand.

" I wanted to give you something as a sort of
keepsake like ; but this is all I've got. It ain't
much, but I've had so many ' breakages ' lately,
missus says there's nothing to pay this quarter.
I suppose she knows. Anyhow, this is all I've got,
and you're welcome to it. I'll take care of Whispy
till Jack can have him" (the kitten had been be-
queathed to a poor little blind boy who lived not
many doors distant, that it might tend to cheer his
days of loneliness and pain—this fact taking away
some of Lizette's regret at having to part with this
little friend in her affliction). "He'll be safe enough
with Jack ; and they're sure to take to each other,
'cos they ain't either of 'em got no eyes. Mind you
don't turn out of the hospital till you're quite yourself again. Don't let them doctors cheat you into
believing you're all right" (the representative of

that faculty smiled at this compliment). "There's missus a-hollering again; good-bye, and mind you get all right quick—good-bye."

And although the sound of the warning voice was audible only to her own ears, which must have been sharpened by use, the girl turned quickly away. Lizette, however, bent forward with a look of greater interest on her face than it had worn all day, and laid a detaining hand on the fat, be-besmeared arm.

"Is it not the habit to kiss the friends you like at parting?" she said, perhaps thinking of another good-bye which had been far more cold.

Sarah paused, looked in at her with wide-open eyes which, instead of the usual sleepy expression, had a sort of "doggish" dumb look in them.

"I'm afraid I'm not over clean," she said, looking down at herself ruefully—the first sign she had ever shown of being conscious that her appearance was hardly what it might have been.

"That does not matter," replied Lizette, without even smiling at the curious figure.

Sarah took up the corner of her apron, rubbed her face vigorously with it, with the laudable intention, I suppose, of removing some of its ornamental designs—a purpose which was defeated, owing to the ragged apron being in a far worse plight.

This done, she again thrust herself half-way into the cab, gave Lizette's upraised cheek a sort of peck, meant, I suppose, for a kiss; then, perhaps touched by feeling it wet with the tears which would come from the homeless, friendless girl's eyes, flung her arms impulsively round her neck, and repeated the caress with a warmth of which any one who had seen her a few moments before bending over the wash-tub, would have hardly deemed her capable.

The next minute she was left standing on the pavement, looping up a stray tress of hair, of which she always had at least one loose, while she watched the cab slowly retreating in the distance.

It was not until it had turned the corner that she became aware of that cry "to arms," "Sarah! Sarah!" and when she did at length turn indoors in obedience to it, there was what might have been described as a roadway running down amidst the smears and smudges on either cheek.

As she vanishes in at the door of No. 19 Wicker's Row, so she vanishes from this story. She is only a link in the chain which I have to forge. What afterwards became of her I know not. But it is to be hoped, for the sake of those who fear ghostly visitants on this earth, that she outlived her mistress ; for certain it is, so strong was the power of that lady's voice raised in the never-ceasing call of "Sarah! Sarah!" that, no matter how soundly she might sleep, it would not fail to bring some response.

.   .   .   .

Meanwhile Lizette had already reached the hospital to which, through Dr Woodward's kindness, she had been admitted. He had deemed the step necessary, as he feared, unless the case were properly attended to, it would develop some grave symptoms.

In the ward to which she would be carried, the nurses were already preparing for her arrival, making ready two beds, Nos. 98 and 99, which stand a little apart, in a corner by themselves.

In a little while along the street leading to the hospital came two figures—one that of a tall, gaunt, raggedly-dressed man, with a strangely white, haggard look on his face—the other that of a young girl, less poorly dressed, but none the less likely to excite pity. She was very pale, her eyes dull and sleepless looking, her lips drawn now and then between her teeth, as if she was in pain, and it was easy to tell by the way in which she walked, dragging one foot wearily after the other, that the exertion was far too much for her.

She passed at her companion's side, but not close to him — seeming, indeed, to widen the distance whenever she was able—although he from time to time turned and looked fearfully at her, as if fearing her strength might not last out, but she paid no heed. Once he spoke to her, told her to take his arm for support, but she drew back, shook her head, and struggled on.

At the corner of the street some one brushed roughly against her, so that she staggered and would have fallen, had not the tall man put out his arm to save her. At his touch she recovered herself by an effort, and leant against the wall

near for support, motioning him away when he
would have offered her any assistance.

After a moment she was able to proceed, but
still she refused the proffered arm, and they went
on their way as before—one needing help, the
other seemingly ready to give it, and yet far
apart from each other.

Just as they reached the hospital entrance,
the cab containing our heroine drove up, and
from it Lizette Hartzmann saw them part. The
bell had already been answered, and the door
stood open. Without a word or sign the girl
would have entered, but her companion, who had
stood watching her with a fierce, hungry look
in his hollow eyes, sprang forward and laid a
hand on her. She waited, but did not turn or
look up at him, while he seemed to beg her to
say something by way of farewell.

"Say it now, for God's sake! It may be the
last time you'll have a chance. Before you're
well and strong, I may be gone. Don't look like
that. If you're not afraid to die, why should I
be? There's the money for you safe and sure.
It's honest enough, at any rate. Say it now,
won't you?" The fierce light in his eyes grew
brighter, and his face seemed to grow drawn
and seared with a look of mingled agony and
pleading. "Say it, for God's sake! It's only a
few words."

"I can't," was the answer, in a low, almost
stern tone. "I can't say it."

And without a good-bye, or whatever it was

he wished her to say, she passed in at the great door with her burden of suffering and sorrow.

The man waited till she was really gone, then turned down the steps like one in a dream, and the next moment was lost in the crowd.

Lizette saw all this, and wondered what this parting could mean—what were the words left unsaid—wondered if the girl had any more friends that she should refuse to say, " Good-bye—God be with you," to this one who had begged so hard for it.

A few moments later she was in the great big airy ward, in one of the two beds in the corner apârt. The other one was also occupied, and, as she laid her head upon the pillow, she found a face which seemed familiar to her looking at her across the narrow space which divided the two beds. The face was that of the girl who had entered before her.

But Lizette was too weary from her journey, which had taken some time, to notice more than this, and she was too weary even to be very sad when Dr Woodward said good-bye.

The kind old man had done all he could for her, and now left her where she would have every attention and the best advice—in fact, she could not be in better hands.

" 99 is your number," he said, looking down kindly at her. Then turned away, promising to come and see her whenever he had an oppor- tunity.

So when he had gone, Lizette called to mind

how much she owed to him, and how cold and few her thanks had been.

"Never mind," she thought, turning her burning face over on the cool pillow—even so slight an action bringing one of the soft-footed, gentle-voiced nurses to her bedside with a cooling drink,—"I will be more grateful when I shall see him again."

But the good old doctor never received her thanks. Only a few days later he went to where he would receive a higher reward for his good deeds—and they were many—than men could give.

In rescuing from the very jaws of death a poor, little gutter child—who spent the life he had saved in misery and sin, he fell a victim to the disease from which she was suffering. And he who had fought the battle so manfully for many another poor soul — who might, perhaps, have wished that his skill had failed—was defeated and slain when he fought for himself.

His life had been a lonely—some said a cheerless—one, but one, at least, of those whom he had tended, whose suffering he had eased, whose sorrows he had cheered—the little disabled circus-rider—did not forget to pray that he might be accounted sound and able in soul by the greatest of all Physicians.

So died another of Lizette's friends. And now indeed she was alone—for in spite of her good-natured offers, what could Sarah do?

Yes, Lizette was left alone in that great citadel of pain and suffering, where each subject pays silent homage to King Death, to slip down, down the narrow path to the unknown Land which lies beyond, to be snatched by firm, courageous hands and resolute, brave hearts, back from the shadowy portals, or to pass for evermore into the mighty stronghold from which there is no exit gate to earth.

While on the first night the poor little fancy rider lay awake tossing and feverish, a loud cry of agony and fear broke the silence of the night, and woke many a weary slumberer from her rest.

It came from the bed next to Lizette's, in which the strange girl lay. She was asleep, and, no doubt, in her dreams was living over again some scene of terror in her life, for the cry was one of mental, not bodily pain.

The nurses, keeping their patient watch, hastened with swift, silent steps to her, to hush and soothe her, gently and kindly, as a mother would her child.

As one of these—a tall, graceful woman, with a calm, peaceful face—passed quickly by the two beds, which stood apart, her soft, clinging dress touched the foot of each, sweeping from the hooks to which they hung two small numbered cards.

Not noticing what she had done she passed on out of the ward, to call for help to a poor soul whose sands of life were very low.

A moment later, one of the younger nurses, a quick-looking girl, went by, picked up the cards, restored them to their places, and hurried on to her duty.

So passed Lizette's first night in the hospital, and many after like it.

The nurses remarked that no one inquired after her ; no one wrote to her, or sent her any of those little offerings which were showered upon the other patients by loving, anxious friends, who did what they could to ease the weary time of pain and suffering ; no one came to see her on visiting days. She seemed alone and utterly friendless. They did not wonder at it, for they saw many sides of life in this world of suffering of theirs ; and they listened to many tales of sorrow and bitterness, and knew how much misery was possible. But they pitied her because she was so young, and were all the more gentle and tender with her because she had no one who seemed to care for her.

They knew that trouble of the mind will stand in the way of recovery of the body, and they tried to draw from her her history, to get her to speak of the sorrow which they fancied was hers, but she would tell very little—nothing, in fact, to give them any clue to work upon.

She was patient always under the suffering she had to bear, never complaining, but seeming weary —oh, so weary! Sometimes she would talk in her sleep, now in her own language, now in broken English ; now mourning some one who must have died not long before, and now telling some one to go away quickly, and yet entreating him to stay —not to go, not to leave her.

But a little later they saw that their help for

the body was not needed. Another influence was at work. Wheels within wheels were turning in that mysterious manner for which none can account.

The two white faces resting on the pillows of those two beds in the alcove were often turned towards each other, as if drawn by the sympathy which the young and friendless and in trouble cannot but feel for each other.

Scarcely a word, save good-morning or good-night, passed between them; but Lizette never turned that way without finding the big grey eyes of the strange girl fixed upon her, as if yearning to speak to her, perhaps to tell the meaning of that cry in the night—the words she would not say to the gaunt, haggard-looking man. Then days of pain, which meant life or death, came to the quiet corner. Fever laid hold with a fiery hand, while to the other came new strength, new life.

Hour by hour the nurses watched and tended them, never flinching from their task, working like the brave, good women that are to be found at such posts, which require a stronger spirit, or at least a more patient one, than even men can boast.

And at length the turning-point came. Consciousness returned, and now weakness was the only thing to fear. With consciousness came thought, and the tongue which had before been silent now gave the poor heart relief.

When the evening was drawing in, the two beds, which stood apart, were drawn closer together, and into one listening ear, in broken sentences, the tale of sorrow so long withheld was poured.

And not too soon, if it was to be told at all. Not many days later, when those around slept the sleep which should end with the morning, the swift, silent footsteps passed down the ward bearing a light burden with reverent, pitying hands.

In the morning there was but one bed in the alcove.

And a few days later this was empty. One of the sufferers had gone out into the busy world to begin the struggle afresh ; the other was where strife and tumult are not, where " the wicked cease from troubling and the weary are at rest."

CHAPTER X.

"SHE'S GONE!"

AND where, meanwhile, was Jerry, he who had promised to be Lizette's friend ?

Two or three days after he said good-bye to Lizette, he had an offer to join a good travelling show, which was being started by an enterprising manager, who had bought up Mr Petman's "props," the owner still being unable to take charge of them himself. Indeed, very little hope was ever entertained of his being on the road again, so completely had the attack from which he suffered, told upon an already undermined constitution..

He was, therefore, left upon the tender mercies of his son-in-law and daughter, the former of whom must, I should think, have been at his wit's end to know how to support this heavy responsibility.

The turn which affairs had taken was any but the one he had looked forward to. He had expected to live upon the salary which he and his wife would receive for their services, until the

time when Mr Petman might give him a share in
the show, which, later on, he (Hermann) hoped to
get into his own hands entirely.

So much he calculated upon gaining by this
marriage. Added to this, there was the report
that Miss Petman was heiress to a good fortune
on her old aunt's death, which might serve as an
additional prop to lean upon. Carl, however, did
not place much faith in it. But it so happened
that matters turned out the reverse to what he
had expected.

His plans about the show were brought to
nought, and he was fast beginning to think the
whole affair of his marriage a most disagreeable
affair—having to work for his relations did not
suit him at all—and Mr Petman seemed to have
known how to spend as well as gain—when a
turn of fortune's wheel befriended him, one, perhaps, of the least deserving of her slaves.

Aunt Betty, *the* aunt—that is, the only one whose
worldly possessions entitled her to be remembered
by her relatives—died suddenly, leaving the whole
of the same worldly possessions—which she would
very much liked to have taken with her if she
could—to her niece, who by a number of little
artifices and ways had managed to make the old
lady believe that she was very fond of her, independently of her money.

At any rate, somehow, the matter was brought
about, and Carl Hermann found himself the fortunate husband of a lady worth as many hundreds
a year as he had formerly received tens from her

father. His pride in his wife, and his own good sense in having married her, revived like magic before the touch of wealth, and he became straightway the most devoted of spouses.

In less than no time—that is, rather sooner than one would have imagined so devoted a niece would have got over her relation's death—the manager's daughter was established in a handsomely-furnished house in St John's Wood, where, with what seemed unbounded wealth, added to a certain showiness of person and manner, the manager's daughter was soon in the full tide of fashion, a very gay star in the firmament of society. Her husband grew more proud of her than ever, and a goodly number of admirers soon made the lady's heart rejoice by the homage paid to her.

Meanwhile, how did Mrs Hermann fulfil her filial duty? Her father, of course, was provided for by her, and if anyone—of course of his old friends—he was not known in society—had inquired after his welfare, they would have been informed that he was as well as could be expected —as well, in fact, as every comfort could make him.

But where was he? Living with his daughter, to be sure. And yet not one of the grand guests who came and went from it ever seemed to know of his existence. You see their rooms were never higher than the fourth floor in the lofty mansion ; they never even so much as glanced up to where the stairs led still upwards. The servants, of course, slept in small low rooms on the top storey.

But there was one room which was tenanted day and night by a helpless, feeble old man, who had only just sufficient strength to crawl from his bed to the arm-chair near the window, from which he looked out upon the busy world of fashion which rolled by below.

His room had formerly been on a lower floor, but it had been wanted for visitors, and he had been gradually shifted higher and higher up until he was lodged with the servants next the roof.

At first his daughter had paid him all the little attentions their relationship demanded, but as the number of stairs between their apartments increased, so also did the distance between their respective positions.

The child was the handsome, rich Mrs Hermann, the father the broken-down circus proprietor, whom nobody knew and nobody troubled about. She drove about in her carriage and pair, gorgeously dressed, surrounded by every luxury ; he was left to the mercy of the servants, who, to do them justice, did their duty so far as they were bound to do. He was not, as might have been expected, very grateful for the services they rendered, and entirely destroyed any pity which one or two of the better-hearted ones might have felt for him, by his savageness of temper and coarse, vulgar manners.

It was hardly to be expected it would have been otherwise. He was not the sort of man to reform his ways, because he was laid on his back and could not help himself. There was a sort of dogged defiance about him which forbade any hope of his developing a Christian spirit.

His life, too, in the little room was not calculated to soothe one who had formerly held reins of power. His only enjoyment—books, and all intellectual enjoyments, were forbidden him—was to sit in his arm-chair—a crippled, almost deformed figure, all his robustness gone, and listen to the sounds of gaiety and mirth going on down below.

It is little wonder his thoughts were bitter, and that when—made aware by some chance word of her ill-filled duty—his daughter, radiant in some grand costume in which she was just off to some high festival, would slip unobserved by her guests up the narrow staircase to his room, that she met with little return for her condescension in having paid the visit, than cross words, ill-natured sneers and jeers, which made the interview anything but an agreeable one.

But we must leave the happy young couple to their gaieties, and return to Jerry. He rather preferred the roving life of a travelling show to remaining in the same dull town, where, now that he had no visits to pay, no sister to look after, the days seemed to go very slowly.

He did not exactly know what good he would do by staying where he was, for the memory of his letter and that last visit to Wicker's Row seemed to have placed an impassable barrier between him and Lizette.

She knew his secret now, and was pained, if not

angry, because of his presumption ; and how could they go back to the old relations, even if " the world " would have let them.

Jerry tried to face the situation bravely—tried to find its bright side, but—I am bound to confess it—was in his heart utterly wretched and miserable.

He tried, for the sake of his work, to keep up an appearance of being the same as usual, and did his best to believe that the opening of the old wound had brought back none of the old smart and pain, trusting to time to heal it again, though never in this life would the scar be effaced.

About this time, too, he was deprived of the friendly intercourse which he had formerly had with his landlady's niece.

I do not exactly know how it came about; but a few days after Lizette left the Row, a story got circulated among Miss Jane's friends, which led to some doubt as to the authenticity of her reported relations with the circus clown. It seemed that in sweeping his room the young lady's aunt discovered the remains of a large quantity of writing paper, which had not been so entirely destroyed as to prevent their being placed together in order to ascertain their contents.

The result was a disclosure which led Mrs Wippington to question her niece rather closely as to exactly how far her supposed suitor had " gone."

The answer she received, not being, as she had hoped it might have been, sufficient to found a breach of promise case upon, she coolly told her niece that she had been a fool, and informed her of her discovery.

Miss Jane's feelings can better be imagined than described. She had hysterics for one whole day —laid on a couch with her back hair down, at least, what of it was her own—and wept " quarts," as one of her boy cousins described it.

At the end of that time, maidenly pride came to her aid. She called Jerry a base deceiver, and sundry other melodramatic names, which would otherwise have astonished him could he have heard them, and decided to turn her attention once more to the barber's assistant.

To this end, that very evening she paid a visit to his master's shop to purchase a pot of bear's grease, a pomade which he had often recommended to her in days gone by—to which days she was going to refer with tears and sighs—lay the blame of the coldness between them on his shoulders, for not having taken a firm " no " for a trembling " yes."

But, alas! how bitterly were her hopes doomed to disappointment. Entering the cutting and shaving saloon, kept (of course) by an Italian (I never could understand why the trades of hair-cutting, umbrella mending, and ice selling seem to be devoted to Italians), she found her *ci-devant* admirer engaged in operating upon the abundant tow locks of a young lady, with whom it was plain to see he was on no ordinary terms of acquaintance. Poor Miss Jane, he only bowed

quite coldly and stiffly to her, and continued
brushing the flaxen locks of the other young lady
with great care, all the while whispering to her,
and seeming quite to have lost his former bash-
fulness.

Miss Jane controlled herself sufficiently to make
her purchase from another assistant, and then
turned to leave the shop at once, and for ever.
She had sense enough to see that her running was
over in this field. But she was not to get off
scot free. Noticing her presence, the baby with
the tow hair looked up into her admirer's face
(such he undoubtedly was), and with a smile of
childlike simplicity, asked some question which
was evidently relative to the glossy coil of hair
which Miss Jane wore beneath her hat, and which
the barber's assistant had formerly professed to
look upon as her own.

Now, however, he gathered his last love's
abundant tresses in his hand with a caressing
gesture, and said, with a professional shake of the
head,—" Oh, dear no — false — all but the top
roll."

Poor Miss Jane, how she managed to get out of
the shop she never knew. She had a dim recollection of seeing the treacherous assistant fling
the soda doctored tresses of the baby-faced girl
over her shoulders, with a murmur of admiration
at the thick veil it made, while she looked after
the retreating figure of the bear's grease purchaser
with a glance of positive horror at anyone being
so base, so depraved, as to wear false hair.

I may say that, all unknown to her, Miss Jane was avenged in this quarter at least.

The continual immersion in soda had, later on in years, when baby-face was Mrs Barber's assistant (her husband never rose), the effect of turning the flaxen locks a brilliant shade of red. In alarm, the lady tried every means to make it return to some more becoming hue, with the effect of making it come out in handfuls, until she became so bald she was reduced to wearing a wig, or going about looking somewhat like a bald canary.

Miss Jane, however, never knew this, and her heart was very bitter when she returned home from Signor ——elli's that night; she determined, however, to bear up, — to invent some story to account for Jerry's (supposed) heartless conduct.

Her aunt, however, saved her the trouble of putting her imagination to work, by telling the truth to a very old friend. The result of this was that Miss Jane suddenly discovered she was very much needed by her family, and departed in some haste to gratify their desire.

The truth was, her aunt's abode was rather "too hot" for her, and so she left. Jerry was rather suprised to hear of her flight, but not being just then given to holding much communication with those around him, he never learnt the truth of the matter, which, perhaps, for his peace of mind, was just as well. For there is no knowing but that in his then unsettled state of mind, the knowledge of what his unreturned love for Lizette

had cost him, rather than have any one endure
like pain for his sake, he might not have offered
himself as a sacrifice for a fault he had not committed—and married Miss Jane.

The saints forbid !

Fortunately there was no occasion for the saints
to trouble themselves, as the banns were never
put up. Nothing just then was farther from
Jerry's thoughts than the idea of marrying. He
had made up his mind completely, now that he
had missed his turn, and he meant to "cut" the
business entirely, and get along through life as
best he could with his old tricks and turns, ready
to wait quite patiently till he got the signal for
his hand-over-hander into the next world.

Meanwhile he tried to take up his old ways just
as he had left them off before Lizette had come
and changed him from what he was, but it was a
hard task, and he had to struggle manfully on.

The worst of it was, that there seemed no end
for him to work, for every one knows how listlessly
we fight when defeat and conquest are alike of
little value to us.

When Lizette should be well again, there might
be some interest in keeping guard over her from
the distance, but till then there was nothing for
him to do but to wait. He had been to see Dr
Woodward, who had wished to hear personally from
him the result of the interview which he had advised
him to have with Lizette, but already the doctor was
sickening with the disease which was to take him
from the midst of his work. He could therefore only

send down a message to Jerry, who went away repeating the No. 99 to himself, and the assurance he
had received that Lizette was well cared for where
she was, and that there was very little to fear.

He would have liked to have gone to inquire himself at the hospital, but it seemed like distrusting
the doctor. Besides, there was the memory of that
" Go away—oh, please go away," and the motion
of the thin white hands, seeming to tell him he
was not needed.

Dr Woodward had promised to let him know if
he could be of any use, or if Lizette should take
a turn for the worse, and had also promised to see
what he could do towards getting her some light
employment when she left the hospital.

So Jerry trusted to him, not thinking that the
enemy he dreaded for others was already over-
taking the old man.

Three weeks went by—a long time when it
means the record of the journey along the narrow
path of sickness ; and as there were no news, Jerry
knew things were going on all right.

A day or two later, however, he began to think
he was silly to trust so blindly to fate. Supposing
the doctor were worse, unable to let him know-
if anything were wrong—supposing the grave
symptoms which he had feared, had developed
in Lizette's case—supposing—Jerry did not wait
for many more suppositions, but, full of fears,
started off to the doctor's house. He reached it
only to hear that the old man was dead.

Jerry was unfeignedly sorry to hear this, for he

knew how good a friend Lizette had lost. But
he did not stay even for regrets, but started off
at once to the hospital, determined to gain some
news of the sick girl, trusting, hoping that the
foreboding of evil in his heart would prove but
the idle fancy of his weary brain.

Why should there be anything to dread? Dr
Woodward had only said there might be something serious come of this second attack,—that
fever was above all things to be feared—but he
might have been wrong.

Yet his heart was beating fast as he mounted
the stone steps of the hospital, and made his way
to a little room where one or two gentlemen were
talking together, and where, at a small table,
busily writing, was a young man to whom he
addressed his inquiry.

"No. 99," repeated the young fellow, pulling a
big book towards him, and running his finger down
the page. "No entry to-day. Must be a mistake."

"No," said Jerry hoarsely; "99 was the number.
I ain't likely to have made a mistake."

"Anyhow, 99's empty now," said the young
man, rather put out at the young clown's tone.
"Must have gone out."

"I tell you she hasn't gone out," said Jerry, going
a step nearer. "Let me look at the book." And
in his agony of fear he tried to seize the volume,
which the clerk drew nearer towards him. "I tell
you," went on Jerry, all his passion rising, "if you
don't let me see I'll—" and he made a threatening
gesture.

The clerk had already turned over two or three leaves, running his eye down them until he came to an entry at the end of one page. Here it rested for a moment, while the colour in his face seemed to pale a little. After a moment, he looked up quickly, glancing to where the gentlemen stood in the corner. "You're no relation?" he asked. Jerry shook his head. He could not speak. "Excuse me a moment," the young fellow said falteringly; "I will speak to Dr Turner." He crossed the room as he spoke, but left the book behind him. No sooner was his back turned than Jerry had seized it and found the place at which he had closed it.

When the clerk came back, followed by one of the gentlemen, who turned quickly on being addressed, he was still standing looking down at the page as if he had been turned into stone. The gentleman spoke to him in a soft, kind voice, but he did not answer, nor even turn his head, only stared down at the words.

"How could you be so careless, Halsie. Have I not warned you to ask all questions, if anything like this occurs, and to send for some one else," said the soft voice sternly. "This must not happen again. It is the one thing above all others to be avoided. I will speak to Mr Drayton about you to-night."

The clerk's face fell visibly. He knew what speaking to Mr Drayton meant.

"He said he was a relation," he faltered, quailing visibly under the stern glance.

At his words, Jerry looked up, closed the book slowly, and laid it on the table.

"I said I wasn't a relation," he said, in a slow, measured tone, very unlike his late fevered utterance. "And it's true I'm not a relation, but—" he paused and looked absently round him, apparently forgetting that his sentence was unfinished.

The gentleman motioned the clerk away, and going a step nearer, laid his hand kindly on Jerry's shoulder.

"No relation," he said; "not a sister or cousin, but going perhaps to be something nearer one of these days? She was to have been your wife?"

"No, sir," said the calm voice again, and a tearless, stony face was turned to the doctor's pitying one. "No, sir, she'd never have been my wife, Liz wouldn't. I'd have died for her, if it'd saved her any pain like she had to bear; but she was much too good for the likes of me, sir. She was a lady, and I—I'm only a circus chap, not fit to brush her shoes. Besides, there was some one else."

And he turned away. The doctor stayed him.

"You are sure there is no mistake. The number was 99."

"Yes, 99; the doctor told me. There's no mistake. I might have known how it'd be. She was too good to stay here. She's gone."

But the doctor bade him stay while he examined the book again and made inquiries of one of the nurses of the ward. All she said, however, only confirmed the report which told Jerry that once again he was too late—too late by nearly a whole week. Lizette Hartzmann, the little fancy rider — his little sister — the girl he had loved better than his life; little Liz and he would never meet again on earth.

Two days before, she who had died without a friend to pay one last tribute to her memory, had been laid to rest in the crowded cemetery outside the town,—in the nameless grave where already had been laid to rest other unfortunates who had been like her—friendless and alone in death as in life.

Jerry did not ask where they had laid her. He only knew that she was dead, and asked no more questions.

"Her turn's over," he said, when the doctor, shaking his head sadly, turned to him again. "Her turn's over. I should like to have took her off. It must have been lonely like for her to go alone." And he laughed—a queer, husky sort of laugh. Then, seeing the doctor watching him keenly, he added, "Don't mind me, sir; it's my way of talking. I'm in the fooling line, you know. Me and she were together a bit in the business, but they've put her on alone now. I couldn't expect I could have a turn along with her. But there, you've told me what I want to know, so I'll be going. Thank you kindly, sir, for doing what you have; and," catching sight of the clerk, who looked sadly downcast, "don't be hard on him. He ain't likely to miss his hold and make a slip again. Give him a chance." And nodding gravely to the man, he went quietly out of the room.

The doctor looked after him.

" If he doesn't break down soon," he said, "there'll be a bad piece of work for some of us."

As the young clown, without another word, passed out of the big entrance door, twirling his cap between his hands, a grey vacant look on his face, he had to stand back to give entrance to a tall, gaunt, raggedly-dressed man, with a white, haggard face, and a strange look of fear in his hollow eyes.

Jerry waited a few moments on the steps, looking absently round him, like a dreamer half-awakened from a dream, only with the consciousness in his heart that the dread he feels is not only a phantom of sleep, but a living thing, which will be for ever with him while he lives.

After a little the man who has gone in after him came out again, looking, if possible, more haggard than before, his gaunt form more bent, the whiteness of his face deepened to an ashy hue, his eyes burning like two fiery coals beneath the overhanging brows — the fearful look in them deepened to one of strange wildness and fear— awful soul-binding fear—of something, he hardly seemed to know what.

In his hand he held a white paper—a small, twisted note, over which his lean brown fingers met with an iron grip, as if it were thus he would like to grapple with his mortal foe, while his drawn lips quivered and parted convulsively — though no sound fell from them.

Moved by a sudden impulse Jerry turned towards him.

"Is she—gone?" He could not bring himself to say the word of deeper meaning. "Is she gone—you came to see too?" he asked abruptly, in the strange voice in which he had spoken to the doctor.

The man did not seem at all surprised at such a question being put to him by a stranger: sorrow binds us all in one brotherhood; besides, he looked rather beyond than at his questioner, as though the query was one which claimed his attention.

"Yes," he said, in harsh, grating tones, which suddenly sank into a hollow whisper. "Yes—she's gone—she's gone!"

So saying, he turned quickly away, burying the paper he held in his breast, and with his torn coat open, so that the piercing east wind played with his begrimed shirt, and racked his attenuated frame. Out he went into the hurry and bustle of the city, not heeding—not fearing the weather, only with that strange, ghastly fear in his heart making him shrink guiltily from every shadow, and start at the sound of every hurrying footstep behind him.

Like a spirit in a world of living beings he seemed. Homeless, friendless in the midst of a thousand souls, an outcast in his own land—among his fellow-men, and this of his own free will.

Ah, what a tale of sin and suffering those pallid lips could disclose; but they are sealed with the seal of crime—a fearful crime; they are silent, and the dark history remains untold, until that Day when all secrets shall be brought to light.

Onward through the noisy streets goes the man of fear, not seeing—not caring whither, till, like a sudden, wordless messenger to his tortured soul, writhing in agony within his quivering body, before him—in his way, as it were—he sees the great broad river flowing on through the darkness, like a long, glittering snake, through the heart of the noisy city, just as the stealthy, crawling serpent sin had crept into his soul and divided it in twain. There it lay—the great rolling river —right before him, to his eyes, and those of every one who cared or had time to look, a second city displayed in its depth.

And in this second city the lives of all those who lived above are reflected—with one difference, —above there is the hum of many voices, the hurry of many feet, the din of life and business,— below all is silence, a silence deep and calm as the grave.

Grave! Who talks of graves?

Why at the thought does that gaunt-figured, white-lipped outcast shiver? Does he recall to mind that unhallowed grave where sleeps a son who died a felon's death—lies in a felon's grave for a crime he never committed?

Perhaps he does, for certain it is that as now leaning low down and looking with those strangely bright eyes into the sluggish depth below, the father of that son sees rising from out the waters, borne along amidst the glare of a thousand lamps —a face he knows but too well.

It is the face of the murdered man, the price of whose life was a death of dishonour and disgrace,—a horror-drawn face of a man who had gone along a lonely road one wintry night years ago—gone with money in his pocket, while in his wake followed one who was starving for want of a few pence, such as from among so much store would scarcely have been missed, yet was refused to him who begged it.

On the morrow the rich man had been found— poor as the poorest beggar in the land—poor as the poverty-stricken wretch to whom he had refused alms—poor in all worldly goods, and in those of heaven, since charity is among the greatest— stiff, stark, and dead.

It was his face—with that fearful haunting look upon it, as the murderer had looked upon it in that deadly struggle—which now rose out of the water,—rose before the eyes of the man who has spent in stealth the money he stole, which to his eyes bore a crimson stain—the stain of blood.

And beside the rich man's face there rises out of the dark oily water and gleaming lights, another—that of him who died the felon's death for a crime of which he was innocent. And yet another—that of a young girl, which had once been fair and comely, but now, alas! bearing like all the rest that look of agony and fear which unites her as a link in the chain of crime. These three faces all looking out from the silence of the other city — the city of shadows. Shuddering and cringing more and more, as he looks in fancy on the darker ones, it is the face of the girl which seems to chain the gazer's attention the more, for, try as he will to tear it from her, over her hangs a strong thick mantle of innocence and love, hiding her from the touch of hands which are stained with blood.

This girl, where is she?

Has he not answered that question to Jerry, saying she has " gone "?   Yes, but he has had too near an acquaintance with death to speak of one who has gone a journey, therefore he answered, " Yes, she is gone."

Gone where?   Gone out of her own free will alone into the big city—gone away from the man who sees in her the one light in his dark life, the one shield between him and the horrors which since that winter's night have crowded round him like so many demons eager to hurry him to the end against which he fights so fearfully—gone because she knows the truth, the truth of the blackest lie that ever man lived out—gone, fled away from the knowledge which it scarce seems possible one so frail could have survived.

He had thought she would die, and he could have borne that, had she never guessed his guilty secret; but that paper he holds in his hand tells him she lives, she knows, and has gone, fled away, preferring rather to fight the battle of life for herself than live beneath the odour of his tainted life.

In those few words on that paper he reads his doom.

" When these people here who have been so good to me give you this, you will know I have not waited for your coming, but gone away alone. You know—you will guess why—you have been to me more than I can tell—but now there is the secret you know of—and I cannot look at your face, and know what I do—and turn away. So I go. They say I am well now as I can ever be. Do not try to seek me. It is best not. When you read this, I shall be many miles away. I cannot thank you for what you have done for me—for what now comes between us God will reward you. Good-bye."

The signature was evidently in the girl's own handwriting—the letter that of one of the nurses —and was so faintly written, and in such queer characters, as if the pen had more than once slipped from the trembling fingers, that he could scarce make it out at all.

" No doubt she would not write the whole name. It is mine, and everything of mine is touched with the crimson stain. She would not be ashamed of it for his sake. ' I have gone away alone. Do not seek for me. You will know why. I cannot look into your face and know what I do and turn away.' She is well now, as my sin will let her be. Another life ruined by it. Is not "— (fiercely)—" one life enough payment for that of a miserly money-grabber? Must three be taken?"

" But," whispered a voice within—the ever-accusing voice, whose tones grew daily louder, "the price that was paid before men was not atonement, but further sin. Yours is the penalty for the miser's death—sooner or later you will pay it. Hers, which is part of yours, is payment for that of him who died instead of you. He was innocent—so is she. So the balance is equal—a life for a life." "I have brought this on her, but she has no word of reproach. She even thanks me for what I have done that was good. I would rather she cursed me, and trod me under foot. ' God will reward me for the rest.' "

At the thought the murderer buries his face in his hands in mortal fear, between which and himself a fair innocent life no longer stands. She is gone, and he is alone with his secret,—his ghostly terrors and horrible soul-searching fancies.

Alone! Yes, he is alone, but for how long? At the same moment he raises his head and listens.

Hark. Who is it hurries so quickly on behind him? Is it some one who knows too?—some one who will take him, put him in the dock, where all those people around will stare curiously at him, and point at him as the man—the demon in human flesh and blood—who stood by and saw his son die for the crime he had himself committed? Will they shut him up in that dark cell, from which none go forth save to die?—from whence he too will go, to have the white cap drawn over his eyes, the rope put round his neck, by which they will hang him till he is dead?

Yes, they are coming—those stern men who

led the son to his death—they are coming now to accuse the father of his double crime—coming nearer and nearer. In a few moments they will be upon him. Already he feels their clutch upon him, which will never be loosened till he pays the penalty of his crime. They come—they come. Oh, the terror of it! Is there no way of escape? None—the hunted wretch stands at bay.

Then suddenly a thought bursts into his mind amidst the rush of fears. Instinctively he gives one swift glance round at the city of never-ceasing toil, ever-dying pleasure,—gives an unspoken adieu to its sin and sorrow, of which he has had so great a share, then turns and glances down, down, far into the darkness, where flows the mighty river.

And there, as ever, from its glimmering surface those three white dead faces he knows so well look up at him.

Dead! Who says that they are dead?

No, no, it cannot—shall not be. In them alone lies his safety—they only can be his shield.

Yes, they can save him—and they shall. His arm, strong as it once was, is not yet too feeble for this task—to snatch them from the dark water of the Past and place them between him and his accusers.

Come then, there is no time to lose. Quick—lean low over the stone parapet while there is no one by to see,—only in the distance those footsteps of the accusers coming nearer and nearer!

Quick! quick!—stoop lower, or they are upon

you! Loosen your hold on the iron rail; you
will need all your strength to drag them up.

Lower and yet lower still; for the footsteps are
nearer too. Haste—in a little while it may be
too late!

So urges the accusing voice, grown from a
whisper into a shrill cry, which is almost a
shriek.

The poor haunted wretch obeys its direction,
and with his eyes fixed on the faces beneath,
holding out his trembling hands to seize them.
He almost touches them. They evade his grasp
—a breath of wind stirs the limpid waters into
a dozen ripples, and in them the faces die away
with a mocking smile. He who would seize them
struggles to regain his hold, since his prize is
gone—but in vain.

He has bent so low, there is no going back now.
A thousand arms, long, lean, white, and bare in the
gaslight, are raised from out the water; they lay
hold of him; he feels them dragging him down
—down into the depth below!

There is a rush of many sounds in his ears,
but his own tongue is tied, and, ere one cry for
mercy can plead for the blackened soul, the end
has come which he has so long dreaded.

All is over. The place he filled is empty space
—the waters flow on as before—now hidden in
shadow, now rippling and dancing in the light,
as though with glee at its latest secret.

And the three faces—where are they?

Gone; and in their stead one only looks up

into the starlit sky—the only witness to the last great sin—the last link in the long chain has been forged.

Thus is the last penalty paid—at least, in this life. There is one more shadow added to the many—the land of silence.

Not many days later, in the cold, grey light of the morning, there are those who bear the stiffened body, and lay it in a nameless grave; for there were none could say who is this last poor soul who has flung his life away into the rushing tide.

There is no clue upon him to mark him as the father of one who died that disgraceful death —nothing, save that scrap of paper so tightly clenched in his cold hand that it is dry and untouched by the water—a paper on which they read those words which tell them what they know already—"God will reward us according to our deserts."

And they know it is true, although they can place no other meaning to the sentence; and turning away, leave the body in its last resting-place, there to sleep until that day when the secrets of all hearts shall be known, and the guilty and innocent judged by the Great Judge, whose judgment, unlike that of man, cannot fail to be the true one.

And Jerry, all unknowing of the existence of that scrap of paper with the few words upon it, went home and began life again — or, at least, tried to.

CHAPTER XI.

LEFT ALONE.

AND now my reader must imagine time to have passed rapidly,—nearly a year to have flown by —a year in which nothing concerning my hero occurred worth noting down.

We all know how smoothly the wheels of the vehicle of life seem to run after the steed of circumstance which draws us, has relapsed from its late bold gallop into a steady sober trot. So it was with Jerry.

The period of his mourning for Lizette (which would last for ever), which followed immediately on his sorrow, was one of dull, unending monotony, as what else could it be when the one joy of his heart had been crushed out, and the charm gone from all pleasure and happiness.

He might perhaps have done like many before him,—have sought to drown his grief when he could not otherwise crush it beneath him ; but even in his dullest despair he remembered that his sadness had to do with one who had never been anything but pure and good, and the thought acted like a talisman, as it had often done before, to keep him from taking the first step downwards. His life then resembled that of the little girl who kept a diary, the record of each day in which was "I got up and stayed up till I went to bed."

He was rather singular in his affliction. He bore it as he had done the earlier ones—silently. He told his tale to no one, asked no pity, claimed no sympathy,—only went on his way, alone and unrebellious, with nothing to cling to, nothing to look forward to, nothing to save him, if he should by-and-by slip. The day of his never-to-be-forgotten visit to the hospital, he threw up his engagement at the Hall of Varieties, and quietly stole away from the latest scene of his sorrow.

When he had started on his journey—when it was too late to turn back, he suddenly awoke from the day-dream in which he had been ever since he had read those fatal words in the entry-book.

"I'm turning my back on him as did it all," he said to himself. "If it hadn't been for him and his lying tongue this might never have happened. I ought to have made him pay. I ought to have thrashed him."

And his eyes flashed a dull, sullen fire, which boded but ill for the object of his thought. It only lasted for a moment, then died away as quickly as it had come, and Jerry sank back listlessly in his seat.

" It'd do no good. It wouldn't bring her back, and maybe it'd worry the little Frenchwoman, and ' she' always loved her. No, I won't go back to do it; ' she' maybe wouldn't like it. But," with a returning gleam of fire, " I hope he'll keep out of my way. I don't want to do him no harm ; but if I do come across him, I won't give my word I'll let him go without having it out."

A day or two after, he joined the Petman Show, the right to use which name had been purchased by the new owner, who was a far more lenient— or, I should say, just and kind master than his predecessor.

His object was to revive all the former glories of the show ; and moved, I suppose, by a sort of instinct which made the old props, vans, and ways seem theirs by right, most of the old company gathered quickly under the ancient banner of the " finest show in the world."

The Signor and his thoroughbreds was the first to join, as young as ever—*i.e.*, as carefully made up, as fond of trying his fascinations on any one who fell in his way, and certainly still as great, if not greater, in the grand Apollo act, from which delightful performance it is devoutly to be prayed that that enemy of old age, rheumatics, may not soon debar him ; the Breaknecks, limp as ever in private, spritely as ever in public ; the Japanese children, fast becoming too big for the trick; Madame Fourteenstone, fatter, crosser, and a worse rider than ever ; the Jelli and Boneless Families, each as deserving of its name as ever; Madame Terrelli, with, in place of the performing poodles, two tame monkeys, which she had bought cheap from an organ-grinder—no little pains (on the part of the monkeys) having been spent on their education ; Monsieur Verte, as much the Signor's rival as ever ; and one or two brethren in the trade whose names have not been mentioned in the course of this history ; Tomtit, as drolly sharp ; Merry-go-round, as dully stupid ; Here-we-are-again, as much a combination of the two as could have been found. All followed one after the other, till at length the show, which so lately had been on its last legs, seemed restored to nearly all its ancient glory.

" We only want Jerry and Epsom, and we'd be in prime condition," remarked Will Breakneck one day as he stood in the ante-room, and looked round at his old friends with a watery—his brother said whisky-and-watery—smile. He thought of the little German girl, but remembering that night at Greyton, knew it was useless to think of seeing her amongst them again ; and his not unkindly but rather too soft heart was sorry for her trouble. " We could do without all the rest who like to stay away, but Jerry and Epsom would be the finishing touch."

Most of those round him disputed hotly the desirability of the jockey's presence, but all agreed that that of Jerry would be very accept-able—the wit of the show, as Will remarked, being rather at a low ebb.

The next day, to their surprise, their wish was

gratified. When the performance was going on, the young clown walked quietly into the ante-room. Instantly he was the centre of a group of friends, who all accorded him a hearty welcome back into their midst, and plied him with questions as to how he had fared since they had last met.

Somewhat to their surprise, their former favourite received their overtures of renewed friendship very coolly, evaded most of their queries, and seemed to wish they would leave him alone, and let him go his own way.

Leave him alone! Although at the time his old pals put down the strange alteration in his manner to his being out of sorts, or subject to one of those fits of depression which will occasionally affect the spirits even of such merry individuals as clowns, and took the hint which was implied rather than given, they soon found that it was in fact the motto which Jerry seemed to have made his own.

He seemed to want to be left alone entirely,—to be allowed to go his own way in his own way, but not his old way. It did not take long for it to be discovered that something was materially wrong with him. A change had come over him since last he had been among his friends — a change so great that it hardly seemed possible that this grave, silent, almost taciturn man, who came and went about his work like one in a dream, could be the same gay, light-hearted young fellow who had once been the life of the whole show. He rarely spoke to any one of his friends ; slipped away as soon as his turn was over, and was not seen again until the next day, when the time came for his appearance. He was always punctual, always ready to give a helping hand if it was wanted, never gave any trouble in his conduct, but was all in fact that a manager could wish.

But his old pals could not make him out. They tried to discover what was the reason of the transformation, but in vain. Whatever the cause had been, the effect was such as to awaken their sympathy, rough as it was. They agreed among themselves that something was wrong, that he had had a knock-down blow of some sort, and agreed to do their best to pick him up again.

But they did not know how difficult was the task they had undertaken. They, one and all, failed entirely to re-establish their former footing with the young clown. He gently but resolutely resisted all their efforts to draw him out of the shell of reserve into which he had crept, evaded their good-natured attempts to get him to join them in some pleasure, hoping by it to liven him up a bit, and resolutely kept himself and his unknown trouble to himself.

Finding this—and that not only was it fruitless on their part but also on his—seemed to have the effect of sending him farther and farther within the fortress of reserve in which he had established himself, they decided that the kindest thing they could do was to "leave him alone" as he wished. They did so, but not a few of them watched him when he passed among them with stooping figure, grey-looking face, and dull, hollow eyes, and shook their heads half pityingly, half meaningly.

He seemed like a man suffering from some inward disease, which was slowly and surely eating its way into his system. Yet he never looked unwell, save for his white face and rather slow walk, and never complained, although Mr Winter, the manager, often looked apprehensively at him, as if afraid he might give way suddenly, and asked him if he felt all right, pressing him kindly to have something to freshen him up a bit.

He always replied that he was "all right," and declined a "freshener," and went through his work quite as well without it. The only thing noticeable about his manner was sometimes when he was in the ring, he would look round him quickly, and put his hands suddenly to his eyes. He said his sight was not so good as it had been, and that the lights dazzled him.

In the ring he was as great a favourite as ever. There was a change in his performance—as great as that in his usual bearing in private. But that in public was rather looked upon as for the better than otherwise. Formerly he had, as we know, been one of the quickest, most brisk of his tribe; now it was his very slowness, his sort of sleepy stupidity, which made him seem even more droll than before.

" He's a — funny chap," was the general verdict. " What I like about him is, he's so jolly cool— looks so infernally ' looney,' you can't help roaring."

I suppose he found that the new way increased the favour in which he had formerly been held, for he stuck to it closely, nay, day by day, seemed rather to do the part to greater perfection, to get more quiet, more stupid, more solemn (I think a little less clear sighted), till at length it was generally agreed by the rest of the company, " that, after all, he knew what he was up to," judging by the applause which always fell to his share ; the peals and roars of laughter which greeted his jokes and tricks ; and the hearty calls which almost nightly demanded his re-appearance, all of which signs of public approbation he received with a stolidity,—a sort of dreaming solemnity, which made his very presence appear doubly droll.

His engagement at first had only been for two or three months, and when Mr Winter, finding how great a favourite he was, offered to give it some considerable extension, adding as an extra inducement a bigger " screw" than he had ever been given the chance of before, Jerry told him quietly not to mind about the writing business— so long as there was a bit of the old show left, he (Jerry) would stick to it ; and as to the screw, Monsieur Verte, who had lately been caught in the bonds of matrimony, needed the extra tip more than he did.

I suppose he was quite content with being the

funniest clown out, without needing any further
reward for his services. And yet he did not seem
to take much account of the favour in which he
was held. He would come from the ring after his
third recall, as quietly as if he were deaf to the
roars of applause and laughter which had each
time greeted his appearance—a piece of conduct
which caused some discussion among his fellows.
Some—for his strange unsociable ways, and perhaps his public favour, made him a few enemies,
of which fact he seemed to think as little as of
the show of good nature of his friends—some declared it was his conceit which made him treat
the matter so lightly ; but others repudiated the
idea, calling to mind that he never "took" a
"call" unless Mr Winter gave him permission,
which the manager was only too happy to do ;
indeed, I do not think the audience would have
allowed him to refuse, even if he had wished to
do so.

Will Breakneck, who had a strong liking for
Jerry, defended him warmly at all times, and, so
far as he was able, exerted his influence to guard
him against any annoyance which his strange
ways and popularity might cause him to have
been subjected to—once went so far as to declare
that he did not believe Jerry cared a "rap"—
whatever that might be—whether he was hissed or
cheered, a view which the young clown's singular
manner certainly tended to support, but which
was scouted entirely by the Signor, who living, as
he openly declared he did, upon the smiles of

those who admired his performance, could not deem it possible that any soul, even that of a circus clown, could be so dead as not to respond to the invigorating influence of such a profusion of food.

I fancy, however, Will Breakneck was right, for to the worst and best houses alike Jerry was just the same. Never elated, never downcast, but always very quiet, the dreamy preoccupation which made him the drollest fellow in the ring making him the most incomprehensible fellow out of it.

Matters went on like this for some length of time. Everybody shook down into his or her old place in the show, and Jerry's oddity ceased to be remarked, so easily do we get accustomed to eccentricity, calling it habit.

No one for a moment connected the change in him with the little fancy rider. They thought his defence of her on the last night at the People's Gardens was due to his fearless nature, which would not allow him to stand by and see the innocent suffer for the guilty. Lizette's name was never mentioned before him by his companions, for two reasons. Firstly, her place had been filled up, and out of sight means only too truly out of mind. Secondly, he was so rarely in any company at all, that if any allusion had been made to her, he was not likely to have heard it. She was dead to him, to all the world; and he was mourning her as only an honest true heart can mourn over a sorrow which no earthly joy can heal,—very different from the outward expression of grief, which means the putting on of black clothes and laying freshly-bought flowers upon the newly-made grave.

One name, however, there was which did fall upon his ears now and again. The jockey, who having been one of the most "flash" riders and disagreeable companions in the show, seemed to have made himself remembered. Whenever he was spoken of, that strange subdued light would come into the clown's grey-green eyes, and he would say quietly to himself,—

"I hope I sha'n't come across him. I shall have to do it—he deserves it; but I don't want to hurt him, for 'she' wouldn't have had me."

The next moment the light and animation would die away, and he would be the same strangely silent dreamy-looking man as before.

Matters went on like this, until one day late in summer, what Jerry had hoped might not be, came to pass. Mr Winter had been going the round of the various shows to see whether he could pick up any recruits, as his own was on such a fair road to its old prosperity that he had hopes of obtaining an engagement at the People's Gardens, M——, during the following summer season.

To this end, therefore, he looked out for novelties, and returned to the show seemingly very satisfied with his trip.

Later on, the novelties arrrived, in the shape of a gentleman who ran up a sort of corkscrew stair-case without any stairs, on a big gold ball; a lady who went to much trouble and danger in order to do

on a slack-wire what she would have accomplished
far more easily and gracefully on *terra firma;* a
youth who could assume any attitude on a chair
but that for which this piece of furniture was in-
vented; a young lady who made a great to-do
about walking head-downwards by means of loops
attached to bars suspended from the ceiling;
and sundry other individuals who seemed most
obligingly bent on breaking their necks for other
people's amusement.

Most of these were recognised as old friends by
the Petman company, and fell into their places with
great alacrity; but the last arrival was hardly
greeted so favourably. When it became known
that Epsom was expected, the majority of the
company politely wished he would stay away.

This, however, he did not do, and one day when
Jerry entered the ante-room, he found the jockey
already there. He did not notice our hero, who,
for a wonder, instead of walking off at once to his
dressing-room, stood looking at him. He was, it
would appear, not at all touched by being among
old surroundings again, but was lounging up
against one of the supports of the tent, watching,
with an amused sneer, the evident trepidation of
the groom who was now saddling Daredevil—a
task of no small difficulty and danger, if that animal took a fit into his head to be at all obstre-
perous. By his side, also watching the operation,
was a thin, faded-looking little man, shabbily
dressed, and with a restless sort of air about his
movements which attracted attention. He seemed

to take some interest in the horse, and presently
made some remark about him to his master, which
led to a warm discussion, in which it would seem
Daredevil's merits were being backed against some
horse of which the stranger had a higher opinion.

" Bah ! I will tell you," said the latter, with a
careless glance half of contempt, half of doubt at
the horse present, and speaking with a decidedly
foreign accent, " I will tell you he is not what you
would call bad, but I won't take it he'd cut out
Vengeance if it came to jumping. I know a leap
—the Devil's Gate they call it—a leap that 'd do
your beast up entirely. Mine takes it like a bird—
but Daredevil ! Well, I don't deny that he's a
showy beast—it's about all you require for this
work — but don't set him up for better than
Vengeance, old boy, because it won't do."

The tone in which this was said seemed to put
the jockey on his mettle. About the only living
thing he had ever felt any respect—one cannot call
it affection—for, was his horse, and I believe that
was because it was not in the least afraid of him,
nay, sometimes proved itself his own master.
To hear its powers slighted, therefore, roused the
jockey's anger, and the discussion grew warmer,
until some of the grooms who were near were
drawn into it.

Meanwhile Jerry stood looking on with that
strange look creeping into his eyes. Presently he
raised his head, walked to the corner of the tent,
and picked up something which lay on the ground,
and turned towards the group in the corner.

It was a long driving-whip that he held in his hand, and he looked carefully to the thong as he carried it.

"He's come," he muttered—he had a way lately of talking to himself. "He's come, and I shall have to do it," speaking as if he was about to execute some self-imposed task. "I'll do it here, so that they can all see fair play."

He went a step nearer, with the light in his eyes burning every moment more and more fiercely, till they shone like burning coals, contrasting strangely with his painted face and fool's dress. Again he went a step nearer, till he almost reached the group, and could hear the jockey's voice, thick, as if he had been drinking heavily—an idea which the heavy circles under his eyes and the flush on his face certainly supported.

Jerry watched him steadily for a few moments, then suddenly lifted his hand to his eyes, though he could not say they were dazzled by the light now, for the ante-room was in partial darkness.

Presently he looked up, and, walking slowly to the corner of the tent, laid the whip down where he had found it.

"I won't do it now. It's best not. He's drunk, and he wouldn't feel it like he would if he was sober."

Then he stood quietly aside in a corner, waiting till his turn came, seemingly oblivious of the now noisy discussion which was being carried on only a few paces from him.

A moment or two later he was in the ring—as

funny as ever in his queer, stupid, solemn way—
behaving just as usual, only that the lights must
have dazzled his eyes more than ever, for not
once but at least half-a-dozen times he left off in
the middle of some trick to put his hand over his
eyes, and when he removed it, looked round him
in a way which drew peal after peal of laughter
from an admiring audience.

Those who had seen him before declared he had
never been so irresistibly funny as on that night,
and many efforts were made to imitate the half-
surprised half-stupefied look round.

On his way home that night, Jerry was overtaken by two fellows, one of whom was rolling
along with difficulty, swearing he would " be up
to time in the morning " at some place of meeting,
the other seemingly doubting his word, in order
to make sure that he would keep his engagement.

As they passed him, Jerry recognised the jockey
and his friend the shabbily-dressed foreigner.

The young clown looked after them with one
of those same strange looks which in the ring
caused such merriment, hurried on as if to catch
them up, then paused, seemed to think better of
his idea, and when they turned into a side street,
went quietly home to his lodgings. But not to
sleep. Though usually a rather heavy sleeper,
he could not rest that night. But tossed and
twisted and turned from side to side, repeating
over and over again some words to himself.

" It's nothing to do with me. He won't listen

if I go. I don't want to hurt him, but if he has to pay, I can't help it."

And every now and then he would start up in bed and look round him wildly, as if he expected to find some one in the room.

CHAPTER XII.

A DUEL TO THE DEATH.

TOWARDS morning Jerry slept a little—a dreamful, restless sleep, from which he awoke with a start. It was but half-past four, but he got up and dressed, and stole out of the house into the dim grey light of the night which would soon give place to the day. He seemed to have some object in view, for, once out in the air, he set off at a faster pace than usual away from the busy but now sleeping centre of the town towards the outskirts.

The walk was a long one; and the first rosy tints of the dawn were creeping into the sky when at length he was beyond the town, out in the country beyond. Towards the end of his journey he had began to meet labourers on their way to work, carts going to market, and other such early risers.

Of these he asked his way once or twice, they looking not a little surprised at the destination he required to reach. But he paid no heed to their inquiring looks and questions, and went on his way—tramp, tramp, tramp—like a man carrying a heavy burden.

His load was a heavy—none the less so because it was an invisible one.

By following the directions given him, he turned at length down a narrow lane away from the main road, crossed one or two fields until he came to one in which, at the end, a number of people—about half-a-dozen—were already assembled. The little group consisted of men, two of whom were noticeable before the rest. Just such a group as in the days gone by had often assembled in the sunrise, when headstrong passion had lead two misguided men so far to outrage God's laws as to stake their lives one against the other.

But the days of duelling are over now—in this country at least; so the errand upon which these men whom Jerry saw, were bent, could not have been that.

Besides, the two men of whom I speak were not armed, but mounted each on horseback—one a big, well-made man, with a dark face and care-less mien, who bestrode a handsome grey horse—the other, seated on an ugly, long-legged black horse, a shabbily-dressed little man, with a white face, which would have been almost effeminate in expression had it not been for a pair of singularly sharp, restless grey eyes, which the owner fixed intently every now and then on his companion.

The other man did not seem to care for the look, while, at the same time, it seemed to puzzle him. He stole a glance now and then at the shabby man, as if trying to recall where he had seen him before. The rest of the men were standing near a broad, ragged stone wall which separated the two fields, and must have been the remains of some old fortification. Beyond it was a broad ditch.

Jerry, as he tramped over the broad field, could not see all this, but he nevertheless hastened his steps when he noticed the men on foot cluster round the man on the grey horse, and all seem to be speaking earnestly.

He (the rider) did not appear to listen to them with much patience; and when the shabbily-dressed man drew near, and laughed loudly and gesticulated not a little, he turned away from them altogether.

His companion seemed to urge that time was pressing, pointing to the first straggling beams of the sunrise to emphasise his words.

The man on the grey horse seemed to make some light reply, as if doubting he could tell by this; but when a watch was consulted, the supposition was proved to be correct.

The foreigner bowed, shrugged his shoulders, and, turning his horse's hammer head, cantered some distance up the field.

His companion prepared to follow, while the rest of the men tried to stay him, but he shook them off and also cantered up the field.

By this time Jerry was near enough to hear what was said, and he hurried faster and faster over the turf. Once he stopped, fancying he heard voices in the direction of the lane, but no one was visible.

By this time the horses were side by side, and the riders had them well in hand.

" Will you that we go together, or I first ? " asked the shabbily-dressed man, who seemed quite unconscious of the queer figure he cut on his strange-looking steed.

" Go first," replied his companion, smiling disagreeably. " If I break my neck I sha'n't see you break yours. I wouldn't miss such a fine sight for all the money in the world."

" All right. It is as you will. *Au revoir.* I hope you will amuse yourself at the sight as you think," was the shabby man's reply.

He touched his horse, which set off at a momentarily increasing gallop up the field till within a few inches of the wall, a touch of the whip, and over the great barrier went the big beast, its head well up, its long, ungainly legs gathered under it, taking the leap as easily as a bird.

A murmur of admiration broke from the little knot of observers. The daring rider bowed and smiled in reply, then waved his hand gaily to his companion.

" It is for you to ' come on, monsieur.' I will watch and enjoy the sight of what your beautiful Daredevil will do. Adieu—if you are not afraid."

The face of the tall man on the grey horse grew very dark. With a muttered oath, he gathered up the reins. As he did so, a hand was laid on them, and a grey face with hollow eyes looked up warningly at him.

"If you go, you'll go to your death. There's some plot in this. There's not another horse in the world but that black brute can take that leap. You'll break your neck."

"Out of my way, you snivelling fool. Do you think I'm a baby. I not go where that man's gone! —— me if I won't, if I break my neck."

. . . .

He broke his neck.

The grey went at the leap splendidly, in a very different manner to that of its ugly black brother, but just as its rider went to rise him for the effort, the shabby man, who sat waiting calmly on the other side, looked him full in the face. Perhaps in that glance his friend recognised him; perhaps that recognition was not an agreeable one, but for the first time in his life he lost his nerve. Only for a moment; the next, as the horse rose beneath him, he too smiled a dark, diabolical smile, then—before one could say how it happened, before the smile could die away—there was a crash and a dull thud.

It meant that a daring wager had been made and lost. The jockey—for he it was—had fallen with the whole weight of his horse upon him, both crushed into the ditch.

As soon as they were able, the terrified men who had witnessed the scene extricated the motionless figure from beneath the struggling beast, whose terrible kicks and plunges made one sicken to think of the human form beneath.

A doctor was found, who came at once. When he reached the scene of the accident, the tall, massive figure which had lately been so full of life, lay motionless and terribly battered upon the grass, still wet with the morning dew.

The men—his friends—stood round, awestruck and white. They made way for the doctor, and waited in silence his verdict. It was soon given. George Epsom had taken his last leap. Whether death had resulted from the fall, or from the more terrible means—the efforts of the horse to free itself, could not exactly be said; but, whether spared such fearful agony as this last by a mercy which he had never shown in life, the jockey had, by his own rash act, leapt from this world into the endless space of eternity. With that cruel smile on his lips, George Epsom's blackened soul had gone into the presence of his Maker, there, when all secrets shall be known, to give account of his sins.

"How did this happen?" asked the surgeon, looking curiously and not a little suspiciously round him. "What does this all mean?"

No one answered for a moment. Then the shabbily-dressed man, who till now had remained exactly where he had been when the jockey had fallen, moved his black hammer-headed horse a step or two nearer, till its hoofs nearly trod upon the motionless figure on the grass.

"What does it mean?" he repeated, in a clear, distinct tone. "It means, monsieur, that this gentleman and I have long had an account to settle.

Madeline Petite was to have been my wife, but he came; I have tried many years to find him, but have not done so till now. You in your country will not allow quarrels to be settled as we do. If a man ruins your home, you let him go free; we shoot him. It is well, perhaps, your law will not let us fight. It is a game of chance, and I did not wish there to be any chance. Our duel was to be 'to the death.' I had no plan till I found him yesterday. Then, although I have never ridden in my life before, I bought this horse, because I liked his name. I spent all the money I have in the world, but what matter! It was just such a morning as this when she went, just at this hour. We were even. I had no wish to play unfair. Vengeance carried me safely. He is dead. My honour is satisfied. Monsieur Epsom, *adieu!*"

The shrugs of the speaker's narrow shoulders, and gesticulations with his thin white hands, ended in one low bow to the dead man at his feet—the rosy hues of the dawn flushing the faces of both dead and living with impartial touch.

A moment—then, as the little Frenchman replaced his shabby hat upon his head and turned his horse to ride away, suddenly there came a sound of flying footsteps over the dewy grass, and before any one in the little awe-stricken group could hold her back, a woman was in their midst—a little wizened woman, with grey hair hanging loosely from her bare head, and no cloak or shawl round her shoulders to protect her from the chilly air of the morning.

Her face was white—nay, grey—and her eyes full of a wild, awful terror. One glance she cast round her; then, with a cry of clear ringing agony, flung herself upon the body of the dead man—clung to his neck, and implored him to look up, to speak to her, raining on his rigid face passionate kisses, calling the dead to wake and listen to her endearing words. It was Madame Petite. Like the dog which licks the hand that lately struck it, she had come to save the man who had been her tyrant; and finding him dead, herself free, had no word to say against him,—only bitter sorrow for his death. For some moments which seemed like hours, the old woman, who would never try to appear young again, clung unforbidden to the corpse, while her avenger upon the black horse sat and stared down at her, perhaps hardly recognising in her the girl whose cause he had so long and resolutely espoused.

At length he roused himself, gathered up the reins, shrugged his shoulders, bowed low to the kneeling woman, and silently, slowly—like a dark shadow in the golden sunshine—rode away on his black steed Vengeance.

What afterwards became of him belongs not to this history. He is merely a shadow in the background, and he vanishes into the darkness.

Of Madame Petite too we here take our leave, for the courageous, kindly little circus rider was never seen in the ring again.

She lived on through weary years from that fatal morning of her lover's vengeance—a poor half-witted, crazy creature, to whom death's coming at last was a blessed relief.

After she lay at rest at last, friendless and an outcast in the busy world, when a search was made among her few belongings, hidden away—as a treasure or no it was hard to say—was found the certificate of her marriage with the jockey rider, all too late to save her in the eyes of men. In the eyes of Him who knows all, what, I wonder, was the verdict passed upon her? Why had she chosen a life such as she had led to that which might have been hers? Had it been choice that she should have remained an unacknowledged wife—or what was the power which had made her bow even under this yoke to the man to whom she was well nigh the only friend he had in the world? Whatever the secret which had wrecked her life, surely her love was an anchor which might hold her safe in stormy waters. And, remembering this, and since her own lips were sealed—faithful to her trust until the last— let me ask my reader to think as gently of the poor soul as he can, remembering that the mystery of her life remains such until the day when the secrets of all hearts shall be known.

.   .   .   .

The jockey was laid to rest in a little country churchyard near where he fell, without a soul to pay him one last tribute of respect.

As they carried him from the field where he had met his death, one of the crowd who had gathered near stood for a moment and looked into his face, then turned away.

The doctor, who stood near, turned too, and looked after the gazer, then asked a question of one of the men near, to which he received some careless answer about a " queer chap."

" Queer chap! He's something more than queer. If you're a friend of his, look sharp after him or—" The rest he uttered in a whisper.

" By ——" said Will Breakneck, " it isn't as bad as that? I'll keep my eyes open."

The acrobat did so for two or three days, then seeing nothing to alarm him such as the doctor had hinted, relaxed his watch.

It was the evening performance. In the ante-room there was a bustle as of some new arrival; in the ring Jerry was eliciting roars of laughter by his antics, repeating the old trick of looking round more often than ever, each time causing the merriment to rise higher and higher. Presently he happened to glance in the direction of the ante-room. He was first with amusing solemnity going through the old jumping trick, climbing up one of the stands for those who hold the banners, and making grand preparations to a splendid leap, summoning groom after groom to hold the stand in order to make his footing firm.

A dozen attempts he made to take the leap each time pausing and calling another attendant, till he had the whole army to support him. The whole audience was on the tiptoe of expectation, ready to laugh or applaud. He raised his arms above his head and almost made the spring. It was then he glanced towards the ante-room. In an instant his arms fell; one hand dived into his voluminous pocket, and while every eye was watching to see how the trick was to end, something bright glistened in his hold, there was a sharp report, and the clown figure fell face downwards like a log into the sawdust.

The something bright was a pocket-pistol. The mischief to the brain which the doctor had predicted had brought the end—Jerry's mind had given way. He had shot himself.

For a moment—while those around knew not whether this was fun or earnest—some laughing, some starting to their feet in dismay—the horrified officials stood paralysed, perfectly horror-stricken.

Then they seized a banner, flung it over the motionless figure, and bore it swiftly from the ring; he who had so lately entered it in health, whose antics had so lately roused such roars of laughter, lay now lifeless.

The audience conclude this is some new bit of fun, and would like to see the author of it again.

But they may call and shout as loud as they please. Still motionless he lies on the ante-room floor, the something bright clasped in his hand, his loose cotton dress stained with blood at the breast, his large collar sticking up round his white painted face, his eyes looking up straight—up in to the horror-stricken faces around him.

As they raise the banner, the figure which had

stood in the doorway pushes its way into their midst.

Then a cry of " Jerry " echoes above the murmur of voices. And if any cry on earth has power to wake the soul that sleeps, it is this one ; if any touch call him back to life, it is that upon his face ; for it is a voice which he has so sadly missed as silent for ever, which calls him back to life, calls him back from the grave.

CHAPTER XIII.

IN NEW STRENGTH.

But Jerry did not die. He lived—lived to wake from the sleep which was so much like death—a sleep which brought him back not only to life—but to reason.

Yes, the evil of which the doctors had hinted was the gradual overthrow of the brain power. Ever since that visit to the hospital, the mischief had been going on, slowly but surely, the canker eating its way into his system, till it had seemed nothing could stay the evil. But God had been merciful to one who all his life had had mercy. Just as the evil was on the point of triumphing, help had been sent to the fevered soul. One risen from the dead as it seemed, appeared to bring back thoughts to the vacant mind.

And that thought brought the act which, prompted as it was by a will which was not accountable for what might come to pass, belonged to the demon which was rising within him, threatening to overpower him.

It was the signal for the battle to commence, but the bugle sounded not " to arms," but " truce," and Jerry crawled slowly back to life.

It was one fair summer morning when first he awoke to consciousness. He found himself in a big, homely-looking room, in the window of which —sitting so that the sunbeams fell upon the abundance of brown curls which hung in clusters over her shoulders—was a figure which seemed strangely familiar, and yet unreal, with its head bowed over something it held in its hand. What he could not see, for the back was towards him. It was like one which had been in his mind long months before,—before the change had come—the form of one who had long since " gone to rest "— gone where, as he looked with tired eyes upon the apparition, imagining he was dreaming, he wished he might soon follow.

He thought it was morning, and that he was dozing still. He had not the slightest remembrance of what had happened yesterday or the day before, or of any day since his visit to the hospital. He thought that day of bitter sorrow was but a few hours behind ; he did not know how nearly in innocence he had taken his own life,—did not guess how ill he had been,—only felt strangely tired, so that when he tried to wake, he could not.

So he went on dreaming for some moments longer, in his dream watching still the figure at the window, with the bent head, thinking in a sort of listless way that he would like to go on sleep-

ing for ever, if in his sleep the picture would be
for ever before his eyes.

Presently he felt he must get up. It must be
late in the day, for the sun was high in the sky.
He tried to raise himself in the bed, but his limbs
seemed strangely heavy, and refused to obey his
will.

He tried once—twice—but in vain, and then
turned his head slowly—it too felt so heavy—from
one side to the other. Then he saw that what
the brown head in the window bent over was a
letter, a crumpled, well-worn sheet, which seemed
to be perused with great care.

Suddenly the brown head bent lower. The girl
was kissing the written page. It was just then
that he moved on his pillow.

In a moment—even this slight movement attracted the watcher's attention — she started
noiselessly to her feet, hid the letter in the
bosom of her dress, and with a suppressed little
cry of joy turned towards the bed. At the sight
of the grey, staring eyes fixed upon her, a hot
flush as of delight flooded her face, and her hands
met suddenly over her breast, with a queer, half-
foreign, half-childish action, as if to keep down
some excitement.

A moment she stood looking half fearfully at
the white face on the pillow, on which was gradually
dawning a look of wondering, not unmixed with
terror. Jerry tried to put his hand over his eyes,
but the thin white fingers rested like lead upon
the coverlet; he tried to speak,—to cry out, but

his tongue was dry in his mouth, and all his parched white lips could murmur, was a hoarse whisper—one word, "Lizette!"

Then the girl spoke, calmly and distinctly, although her breath came and went quickly, keeping her large, clear brown eyes fixed on the staring grey ones, as if to transfix their glance.

"Yes—it is I—Lizette. You are awake, not dreaming. They told you I was dead, but there was a mistake. I went away myself because—because I thought I was in your way. Hush—do not speak"—as Jerry, full of amazement, tried to utter some sentence. "I know I was wrong; I know all that you would tell to me. I found Smith, and he told me, and I got this letter"—taking it from her bosom. "When I read it, I came quick to find you; but you—you were ill. I was sorry for it—but glad—glad to show you I do not fear what people might say,—glad to be able to befriend you in your trouble, as you did me—in mine. I have watched many days for you to wake, that I might tell you—that I might say to you how much I am happy to be loved by you. It is not for me to say it. You may think me no woman, but, all the same, I have come to ask you, Jerry—to ask you to let me be your wife?"

She paused breathlessly, and there was a dead silence in the room.

Jerry made no effort to speak, only lay like one in a stupor; only staring with great unbelieving eyes into the girl's flushed, earnest face, as, with all her soul in her voice, she stretched out her hands to him, as if imploring him to make some answer to her confession.

As he did not speak, all at once she let them fall to her side, and the colour fled from her face.

"Surely, surely, I have not been mistaken. This"—holding out the letter—"is not a trick, to make me? Oh, no! and yet—"

The clear, distinct voice failed, the brown eyes dropped, and the drooping form made as though it would turn away. Ere it could do so, Jerry roused himself by a mighty effort, held out his arms, and loud as his weakness would let him utter the joyful cry, called "Lizette!"

There was no mistaking the tone or the action; the slight figure turned again, and with one big sob of happiness, the girl was kneeling by the bed, her hands clasping the thin white ones, while her golden brown head rested against the heart which so long had beaten faithfully in her cause.

.   .   .   .

A little later, Mrs Parkins went and found her patient sleeping calmly, while the little German girl watched beside him, holding his hand in hers, a strange glad look in her face.

The old woman watched them silently for a moment, then stole round to the girl's side, and quietly folded her in her motherly arms. She knew the battle was won.

.   .   .   .

From that day, Jerry grew rapidly better, as how could he help it, beneath the never-tiring care of two such faithful nurses.

There was much to tell, and by degrees he knew all, for, once she had surrendered the key, little Lizette opened her whole heart to him,— had no secret from him whom she had learned to love amidst such pain and sorrow. For she had at last learned the lesson of the roses, and in the new deep love of dawning womanhood, left the fond, foolish fascination of her childish heart far behind in the past.

And who shall say this second love was not as precious as any,—far more so than the first, which long ago she had buried away—from its grave rising her new and far better happiness.

The story of the mistake which made her dead to Jerry, my readers will already have understood.

The exchanged numbers were the cause of Jerry's year of mourning. It was the poor, friendless love of the murdered—not murderer— who had died that still calm night. Lizette had heard her tale of suffering; and, strong even in her own weakness, had been like a sister to her; nay, better, like a guardian angel to a stricken soul.

That tall, fearful-looking man, who lies now in the unknown grave of a suicide, knew it not; but into the stranger girl's ear had been uttered those words for which he had begged in vain. The forgiveness for his heinous sin had been at last granted on earth by her whom he had so bitterly wronged. May not we hope that the Higher Power will grant him mercy in heaven?

Knowing, or thinking she knew, that their

friendship might bring Jerry unhappiness in his approaching marriage, and knowing too her own secret only too well, Lizette had decided not to see him again. To this end she had quitted the hospital and the town, as soon and as quietly as she was able, leaving behind only a short note for Jerry, which note, as we know, he never received. It had another mission to fulfil. Lizette's life, after turning her back on Greyton, had been full of those ups and downs which are the lot of the friendless in this big busy world.

But she was fast passing from childhood into womanhood now, and would not let herself be discouraged by any amount of stumbling.

She struggled bravely on, and at length gained her reward. In her greatest need she remembered a friend who she thought might help her. This friend had lived near the People's Gardens, M——. To M——, therefore, she went, but only to have her hopes disappointed, by finding her friend had some time before left the place.

Despairing, and not knowing where to turn, she had turned away on receiving this information, and wandered for some time aimlessly down the streets which she remembered so well.

Passing a house in a narrow thoroughfare, her attention was aroused by hearing some one whistling a tune she knew only too well. It was " Come Lassies and Lads "—the air to which she had so often leapt banners, burst balloons, and otherwise disported herself on the Turk's back. It was a common enough tune, but it recalled old memories, and she turned to look carelessly at the whistler. Perched on a window-sill of the house before which she was passing, was the big, ungainly figure of a young fellow about seven-and-twenty years of age, rubbing away at the pane of glass before him with great and seemingly unnecessary energy.

As he bent forward to get a view of a smeary corner, his face was visible to our little heroine. In a moment she came to a standstill, and forgetting everything but that here at last was a friendly, if ugly, face, she cried aloud,—

"Smith !"

The fellow, intent as he appeared on his work, heard her, and evidently knew the voice.

His merry tune came to an abrupt conclusion ; his window rag fell into the area below ; his whole body was very nearly following, while he stared at the owner of the voice in amazement. Then he flung up the window, sprang into the room, and the next minute was out on the steps, holding the hand which Lizette held out to him tightly within his own, while he gabbled out question after question in the most confused manner, without waiting for any answer.

Suddenly he paused, and before she knew where she was had dragged the little fancy rider into the house, left her in the hall, dashed headlong down into the lower regions, and returned with missus, as he called her—she being none other than our friend Mrs Parkins.

How Smith came in her service is easily ex-

plained. The day after Lizette's accident, with
a dim idea in his mind that he ought to know
what had happened, the faithful slave had started
alone to find the man who had "shaken him by
the hand and been kind to him." By dint of
great perseverance, wonderful in one such as he,
he had at length reached M——, only to find
Jerry already started off on his search.

Smith had been in despair, not knowing how
his self-imposed mission was to end,—which way
to turn, what to do, where to go. His friendless condition had touched Mrs Parkins' motherly
heart, and she had offered him the place in her
household which had been left vacant by the hero
of the Jacob's ladder *versus* Jerry's exploits having bettered himself — contrary to the dismal
prognostications of his Sunday-school teacher—
Smith had been rather bashful and shy at first.
It was truly a pitiful sight to see one who was
a man in years, little more than a child in ways.
But he had gradually thriven under the widow's
care, and become a "boon" to the lodgers, who
had hitherto suffered not a little from the shortcomings of the various errand-boys who had had
to do with the establishment. He was quiet, and
at times excessively stupid, but he was faithful
to the core, and everyone could trust him—a new
trait in one of his order. He improved in health
too under his new mode of life, and when Lizette
saw him cleaning windows, was well and strong-
looking to the poor, miserable-looking chap he
had once been.

The widow was not a little proud of her *protégé* —and he in return worshipped her, nay, more, he loved her with that dog-like sort of affection which was such a strange attribute of his character.

But for the little fancy rider he still kept the first place in his heart, and his joy at seeing her again was unbounded.

Mrs Parkins, too, was very happy at the lucky recognition, and welcomed Lizette to her motherly heart right gladly. She made her there and then a prisoner, kept her for that day and the next, and for many after that, inventing some idle excuse for detaining her till some plan had been formed for getting her work till she should be strong enough, as she soon hoped to be, to return to the ring.

I think this kindness was prompted by the remembrance of that secret concerning Jerry and the little fancy rider, which in a burst of confidence the groom had divulged.

In time this reached Lizette's ears. Her feelings can better be imagined than described. What could she do? Nothing but wait until fortune should befriend her, and bring to light the meaning of the tale, and Jerry's after behaviour.

She had changed—she wondered now why the transformation had been necessary—why should not he?

And while she asked herself this question, and waited, fortune—or rather, I should say, Providence—befriended her. She wrote, now that she was settled, to her old friend Sarah—sending now and then a little present, in return, she said, for many kindnesses, and for the little flat pincushion which she still had safely. In reply to this letter she received one which informed her of the well-being of little Whispy—who was perfectly happy with Jack, who had gone to live with an aunt in the country who had taken pity on his helplessness—and forwarded to her a note, very crumpled and dirty, addressed to her, and which had been found behind the hat-stand during a grand turn-out at No. 19 Wicker's Row.

This letter was the one which Jerry had set so much pains upon the night before he said good bye for ever, as he thought, to Lizette.

On at last receiving it, could she to whom it was addressed doubt any longer that she had wilfully deceived herself? Without waiting to do anything but secure Mrs Parkins' protection, she had set off to find Jerry, putting aside all false pride, in order to clear up what must have been to him a very dark mystery.

The search was a difficult and long one, but at last it had an end—in no less a place than the old ante-room of the Petman Show.

Lizette had arrived just as Jerry's turn was going on, and breaking away from those who would have welcomed her and plied her with questions and congratulations on her return to health—never guessing her errand—she had peeped between the curtains at her lover in the ring.

The result of his catching sight of her face,

which seemed to him more real than it had ever
been in haunting him before, is already known.
The good also which came from evil I have
already detailed.

And so Jerry must needs live and not die,—
live to be happy at last after much pain and
sorrow. And truly it seemed, when health returned to his weakened frame, that nothing was
now wanting to complete the chain of content.
He could scarce believe sometimes even now that
he was not still dreaming—so much too good
to be was the great change that had suddenly
come over his life, turning the shadow into sunshine which should never fade away—sunshine
so bright and glorious that the past dreariness
seemed like part of a hideous nightmare now over
and gone for ever.

And truly indeed did the present blot out the
past, nay, take its place, for all seasons were
alike to Jerry if in them Lizette was the same
to him.

The change in her was what fascinated him the
most. It was little wonder he imagined himself
dreaming when—with the memory in his heart of
the dark days when she had seemed entirely
beyond his reach—when he thought of her as the
pale, sickly little seamstress—she stood before him
once more the Lizette he had first known her.

Yes, the old Lizette; alive, well, strong, and
fair and sweet as ever, for health and time had
done much to obliterate the work of that cruel
fall into the flames. A small portion of the scar

still showed beside her ear, and would never be entirely removed, but the clusters of soft brown curls, which once more as of old fell over her forehead and neck, served to hide the rest. And one forgot even so slight a disfigurement, now that the once pinched, pale features were restored to their former soft roundedness, the flush of returning strength blooming softly in them ; the old flash and sparkle returned to the beautiful brown eyes ; the old vigour and grace to the once languid heavy limbs.

Truly a merciful change to have the old Lizette thus risen from the grave.

Yes, the same Lizette, and yet not the same, for the child during the days of trial had passed slowly into a woman's riper years—the bud had slowly developed into a blossom. Now that its inmost leaves had opened neath the sunshine of a true honest love, its golden heart was revealed at last, and would never again be hidden. So now there remains nothing but to ring the wedding bells, and to leave the two thus happily brought together to begin their new life.

But before we do this, in the gallery to which I have done my best to introduce my reader, there remains one picture yet to be shown.

CHAPTER XIV.

FEARFUL STILL AT FIRST—THEN PERFECT TRUST.

TIME had passed quickly, and once again we find Jerry so far recovered from his illness as to look forward in a little while to being at his old work. He has planned that Lizette and he shall both make their reappearance in their old places in the Petman Show upon the same day—a day which they looked forward to and spoke of long before it was near. Before it came, Jerry had been wont to say the little fancy rider would be Lizette Hartzmann no longer; and she had laughed her old gay, merry laugh because he had been sorely afraid Lizette Bolton would not sound half so well.

"What matter," she had said, quitting her seat where she sat beside him working, for she was still very handy with her needle—quitting her seat to stand upright before him, with her hands resting on his shoulders, her beautiful eyes, soft and true, looking down into his as he had once never dared to hope they would ever look. "What

matter if it is a funny name?   I like it—did I not
ask for it myself?"

She used often to speak shyly of her little
speech to Jerry when he first realised that it was
truly her, and no ghost, who watched beside him,
—the speech in which she had simply but earnestly
offered herself to him, to be the wife he would
have made her long ago, but for that straying from
the path into one of the narrow ways which led
to nowhere.

But from that time she never spoke of her mistake, as she called the little romance of her girl-
hood.   She seemed to wish it entirely forgotten—
to look upon it as part of the dark dream which
she and Jerry had dreamt together.   They were
awake now, and the reality made all other idle
fancies forgotten.   So Jerry, obedient to her
slightest wish, did his best to forget it, although
I fear there were times—times when Lizette seemed
more than ever her old self—the self who had
dreamed the other first dream of love—when he
feared if he was right even now to claim as his own
so precious a jewel as this sweet, fair little ruby.

He was afraid of his own happiness, like the
great big clumsy fellow that he was.

He did not know the tale of the love which had
been so willingly given him ; he did know how,
day by day, it had struggled to life, like some
beautiful flower—first a tiny leaf, then another and
another, till gradually the bud had come and
opened, slowly but surely, into the fair sweet
blossom which had so frankly, so—oh, so willingly

been put into his hand, a trust of which he should have had no doubt. And yet can we be angry with him for being fearful of this great joy which seemed too good for him? The light of day dazzled his eyes after the darkness of the night.

His own love he knew was true as steel. It had been tried by many hours of patient waiting. But hers—was it gratitude or love?

He often asked himself the question, contrasting himself as he knew he was, with her as, always patient, gentle, and winning, she tended him in his sickness, seeming to have no greater wish than to be to him in his trouble what he would have been to her in hers.

But now that their positions were reversed, a change had come over Jerry's feelings. He who had before been willing to give all,—love and life to the poverty-stricken little seamstress—felt he could not take from Lizette the counterfeit coin instead of the real. Now he had got a part, he was not content—he wanted all. Once he would have done much for merely gratitude; now he had that, it was all too little to satisfy him,—he wanted love—pure and unalloyed love. And he doubted if he had this, —doubted, although in every hour of the day, in every action, every look in those glad, honest brown eyes, she whom he doubted, fearing his own happiness, gave him some proof, which he was too fearful to accept. And then, when he had at last resolutely turned his back upon the shadows,—his face to the sunlight suddenly, no shadow, but a real presence, rose up in his path

to bar his way upon the road to perfect content.

One day when he and Lizette were strolling
through the town—obeying the doctor's orders
to get as much fresh air and exercise as possible
before once more settling quietly down to work—
Lizette looked up, to find him gazing earnestly
into her face, with all his honest love shining in
his eyes.

Perhaps it was the expression in her face which
called it there, for she was looking more than
usually bright and happy, because of the doctor's
good report of Jerry that morning.

"Miss Hartzmann," he had said, shaking her
warmly by the hand, "I say good-bye for good
to-day. There is no need for any more physic for
this young man. I leave him in your care, and I
know I can't do better. If all my patients had
such nurses as you, there'd be less work for us
poor doctors."

With that he had shaken Jerry warmly by the
hand, and wished them both much happiness, for
of course he knew how matters stood.

After he had gone, they had set off quietly for
their walk, in obedience to his commands, without making any comment on his words, but as so
far the walk had been a silent one, I fancy they
were far from forgotten.

Indeed, as proof that they were not, when
Lizette looked up so inquiringly into Jerry's face,
he drew her arm closer within his, and asked
suddenly —

"Liz, dear, don't you think it's time we thought about your being made Mrs Bolton—that is, if you've set your heart on it?"

He laughed as he spoke—a merry, gay laugh, such as brought an answering smile to the little fancy rider's happy face.

"I have what you call set my heart on it, so do not think you will laugh me out of it. I daresay I'm silly, but—" She paused, then dropped her light tone, and with a soft, tender look on her face, said softly, "I'm ready, whenever you say to me, 'Come.'"

The word was almost on Jerry's lips, but it was not uttered. Even as he was about to speak, someone in the crowded street—a tall raggedly-dressed fellow—brushed awkwardly against Lizette.

She looked up suddenly, then Jerry felt the little hand on his arm tremble slightly as she drew closer to him as if for protection.

He, too, looked up, to find himself facing—none other than the ring-master, Carl Hermann.

Yes, it was indeed him, though so altered from what he had once been that it is little wonder that for the moment Jerry hardly recognised him. He was no longer the spruce, gentlemanly-looking young fellow whose handsome face had been so often admired, but a shabbily, carelessly-dressed man, who bore upon him the traces of a life which had evidently been anything but an easy one.

He was, it is true, handsome still, but bad living had done much to hollow his cheeks, dull his eyes, and sharpened the once regular features.

Truly times had changed, and he with them. He had lost his old graceful carriage, and slouched along with his head down, dragging his feet after him in a slipshod sort of way, which told that he had to pay for his pleasures, now they were passed. It would seem, too, that he had lost his old courteous manner and usually placid temper, for when he brushed against Lizette, he made no apology, but passed hurriedly along, muttering something which sounded very like an oath.

For a moment, on seeing him, Jerry stood motionless, then, moved by a sudden impulse for which he could not afterwards account, he made a step forward, and before Lizette could stay him, had called the ring-master by name.

He turned, and paused rather unwillingly; but when he saw who it was accosted him, retraced his steps quickly, and passing Jerry's outstretched hand, held out his own to Lizette, saying something in German.

His little countrywoman drew back.

"It was Mr Jerry who spoke to you, not I," she said, with the colour coming quickly to her face, and her hold on her lover's arm tightening.

At this Carl Hermann gave her a searching glance out of his grey eyes, and turned to Jerry, greeted him coolly, and in quite his old grand manner. The two—for Lizette would not join in —stood for some moments talking in a dilatory manner about how things had gone since last they had met.

"I've been unlucky," the ring-master said, playing with his stick. "Never got on but badly since the show went smash. The money all went like blazes, and this is what I've come to."

And he smiled cynically as he looked down at his shabby clothes.

"And Miss Rosa—that is, your wife," said Jerry.

"My wife—I am a widower," replied Carl, while the smile hardly died away from his lips.

"A widower!"

"Yes. It's nothing to look so very surprised about. Rosa died three mouths ago."

There was silence for some time, then Jerry asked after Mr Petman.

"The old man? He's dead too. Died while we were at St John's Wood—the night that—that is, the day that the last of the money went."

A few minutes later, the newly-met friends parted; but for some moments after he had turned away, the ring-master stood looking after Lizette and Jerry, as, arm-in-arm, they passed along the crowded street.

I wonder whether it was because the way was crowded that for the rest of the walk Jerry was rather silent. He resisted all Lizette's efforts to return to their former happy intercourse, and the conversation which the recognition of Carl Hermann had interrupted, was not resumed. Lizette had said, "I am ready," but he did not say "Come."

On the morrow, Lizette, having some work to finish, Jerry, as he sometimes did, but not very willingly, went for his walk alone. When he

returned, he said he had again met Hermann.
Lizette made no comment.

On the day after, Lizette pleaded the same
excuse, and the young clown's walk was again a
solitary one—at least, part of the way—for the
rest, Hermann overtook him, and walked a little
distance with him.

Again the next day, the day after, and for some
days later still this happened, Jerry starting off
alone, but usually picking up the young German
on the road, who became his companion for the
rest of the way.

One morning, just as together they reached the
former's lodgings, it began to rain heavily, and
Jerry asked Hermann in to wait till the shower
was over.

Lizette was sitting in the parlour at work when
they entered together. She greeted the visitor
very quietly, and in a few moments, saying something about wanting more cotton, left the room,
and did not return until some time after the rain
had ceased.

By that time Hermann had gone. But the next
day he went again, after his walk with Jerry,
which had now become quite an established thing,
Lizette being too busy to make one of the party.
and again, two or three days later, always at
Jerry's invitation.

At first Lizette usually made some excuse for
leaving the men together; but one day when Jerry
rallied her, laughing, on running away, she returned to her seat, and went on quietly working.

From that time, she never made any more ex-
cuses, but whenever the visitor arrived, treated
him as she would any ordinary friend, though
sometimes when Jerry would look her way, as
he did very often when he imagined she was not
looking, he would see a troubled look in her eyes
as she bent over her work, and if he spoke quickly
to her she would start, and the colour come to her
face.

Ah! there was mischief abroad, and each felt
the shadow was on them, but had no power to cast
it off.

So the days went on, each one bringing together the little German girl and her former
lover—each one seeing that shadow between
Jerry and his love grow darker—each one passing
without the question being answered,—the one
little word "Come" that had been left unsaid,
being uttered.

And then the end came.

It was the night when Jerry and Lizette were
to go amongst their old friends again,—to go back
to their old work, to be in the ring once more,—
the day when Jerry had once spoke of how he
would introduce his wife to his comrades.

But this would not be now. When the time
came for starting, it was not a duet but a trio
which set out for the show. Carl Hermann had
talked much about the double *début*, and declared
his wish to witness it. On the evening fixed, therefore, he arrived, bringing with him a beautiful bunch
of white roses, which he presented to Lizette with

some of the pretty compliments he had been wont
to pour into her ear in days gone by.

He spoke in German, and the sound of the dear
old language brought a look of pleasure to his
little countrywoman's face, which two pairs of
eyes noted only too quickly.

The next moment she turned quickly to Jerry,
appealing to him as she had grown to do in
everything lately. Once there had been no need
—he had always been only too ready to advise
and help her in even the slightest way.

Now when she asked, "Shall I keep them,
Jerry?" he thought he noticed a sort of timidity
in her manner; and, while he answered lightly,
turned away to hide the look of yearning which
he knew had come all unbidden into his eyes.

So she kept the roses, and thanked the giver
warmly.

A little later, the show was reached, and the
two performers each went a different way to
their dressing-rooms, while Carl Hermann waited,
lounging in the ante-room.

It did not take Jerry very long to perform his
toilet as a rule, but on the night of which I write,
owing to his being rather more particular about
his appearance, or rather more preoccupied than
usual, he let the time slip by until he was afraid
he should not be able to have the chat with his
friends that he had promised himself before the
performance.

Accordingly he made his way hurriedly to the
ante-room, and lifting the curtain aside was about

to enter, thinking it empty, when the sound of a familiar voice made him suddenly pause.

The voice said,—"Lizette, Lizette, don't turn away; you know I always loved you, only I was a fool. I only married Rosa for her money. I swear it. I never loved her—I never loved her! Bah! She was so coarse and vulgar ; only her money would have made me so much as look at her. I never loved her—I only loved you. I love you now, and always have since the first moment I saw you. I meant no harm to you, but I was poor. I could not afford to marry you, to bring you to poverty and misery; but God knows I loved you then, and I shall never cease to do so. And you loved me once. I believe you do so now. Then why should we not be married? I am free, and you— you can be free—if only you will. Come away with me to-night; come with me, for oh, Lizette, I love you so! It was for the best I acted—oh, believe me, it was for the best, and—"

"Hush," interrupted a second voice, clear and distinct after the other's low feverish whisper. "Hush, you have said enough ; I have listened too long. Now, let me to speak. You say I loved you once, but you are wrong. When I was but a little child I had some one in my mind that I loved. He was to be good and kind and brave and true, and loved me because I had love for him. I thought this man was you, but I have found out I was wrong. You were never good, to treat a poor friendless girl as you did; you were never kind, to make her think you cared; nor brave, to leave her to bear the shame all alone; nor true. I ask you are you true now? No; you were not the man I loved, and once I thought there was no man on earth like him; but then I found how blind I had been. Jerry came; and he is good and kind and brave and true, for he has trusted you, and you have deceived him. Do you think if ever I had love for you, even as you say I did, that I could do so now—now when you have been untrue to what I thought a man held sacred. I could not love a man who had no honour; and you, Carl Hermann, have none. I saw what you would do, and I tried to save you; but Jerry was too good. I see now that he was afraid I am not sure of what I would do. He thought I will be his wife because he wishes it—because you were dead to me. You are here, and free, and ask me to marry you, and I tell to you 'No' once for all. I wish he were here that he might to hear me say it, for how can I say it to him? I know he doubts me. And yet— He has not been to me what he was before you came. He is changed, and I cannot tell him to be his old self again, or I shall to hurt him, and I would not do that for all the world. Yes, he has changed; and if, Carl Hermann, you have come between us, instead of loving you, I may come to hate you—to— But— I think you have fallen down enough. I will not to hurt you; only please go now, or I may be unkind—and he would not wish it. Please go."

As Lizette had spoken, Jerry had drawn aside

the curtain, and could see the two speakers,—the ring-master, in his shabby clothes, standing mute, dumbstruck, before the little Fay of Fire, for Lizette had chosen to wear a dress like the one she had worn one day long ago, when first she had found out her countryman was not the good, kind, brave and true man she had believed him. In it she looked more than ever the Lizette of old, fair and graceful as ever, in the pretty scarlet skirt and boddice, her brown hair falling over her shoulders, the glittering helmet, with its nodding plumes, upon her head. But though, as he looked at her, Jerry recalled that day when he stood up in her defence, that memory was soon effaced, to see her now proud and defiant. Her whole figure was alive with earnestness; her head erect, and her face flushed with the quick, sharp energy of her words; her whole bearing a contrast to her fairy costume, but not such a one as it had been before.

When she finished speaking, she turned and motioned with a commanding little gesture of the hand towards the door, meeting the glance of the man who had lost her love and very nearly won her hate, calmly and sternly, so that his own failed.

He tried to speak, but the brown eyes flashed defiance at him, and he turned and left the ante-room.

As he approached the door, Jerry slipped away. He had no wish to meet him,—no wish to triumph. His reward for the past days of fear and doubting had already been given. No, his first thought in this new happiness was pity for his fellow, who so little deserved it.

"He's very down on his luck, poor chap, and Liz was a little hard on him. I suppose he'll be off out of this now. I should like to give him a helping hand for the last time; he's a pal of mine. I know—he may think of paying back what I've lent him. I'll run after him and tell him not to bother."

And darting into the dressing-room, Jerry drew on his long coat over his dress, and darted out into the road in the direction Hermann had taken, knowing he could not have gone far.

Only a few steps and he saw him on the other side of the way, just by a jeweller's shop in the street, before which stood a carriage and pair.

Jerry darted under the horses' heads, and reached his side. As he did so, the door of the shop opened, and a lady came out on a gentleman's arm. He, an old man, padded, beringed and dressed in a style at least fifty years behind his age; she, a big, handsomely-dressed girl, who accepted his lover-like attentions with great condescension.

She was talking in a rather loud tone, and almost before he recognised her face, Jerry knew the voice.

So also did Carl Hermann. He sprang forward suddenly.

"Rosa," he said, laying his hand on the girl's satin-sleeved arm.

She started slightly, and the old-young man

put up his eyeglass, with an air of languid astonishment.

"Rosa, who the deuce is this fellow?"

"Some beggar, I suppose," replied the girl
coolly, shaking off the detaining hand, and stepping
into the carriage. The gentleman followed as
quickly as he was able, telling the footman to pull
up the window.

Hermann again sprang forward.

"I tell you," he said, in a voice choked with
passion, "she's my wife, and—"

"Drive on, Williams," said the lady, drawing
her mantle round her.

The order was obeyed; but the young German's
blood was up, and, furious with rage, ere Jerry could
stay him, he had sprang to the window and clung
to it just as the carriage turned, but lost his hold,
and fell heavily to the ground. There was a
brewer's dray coming up behind, and whether
it was one of its wheels, or that of the brougham
which did the mischief, it was hard to say.

All Jerry knew was that there was a confusion
in the crowded road, a cry, and a sudden rush to
the spot, where Carl Hermann lay crushed to the
earth. It was the work of a few brief moments;
then Jerry found himself by the fallen man's side,
forcing brandy down his throat, while some one
found a cab to convey him to the hospital. The
carriage had driven on; whether its occupants
were aware of what had happened, he could not
tell.

Before the cab could be got, the ring-master,

groaning terribly, seemingly badly hurt, recovered consciousness; but when at last he was lifted into the vehicle, he suddenly ceased moaning, and seemed as if he would faint again.

"Hermann, old fellow," said Jerry, bending over him, "are you hurt much?"

"Yes, I think so; the pain was cursed bad just now, but it's gone all at once. I know what that means. Tell 'em to drive quick, and put me out of my misery."

He turned his head away and closed his eyes, then suddenly opened them, and as Jerry was moving away, laid a detaining hand on his arm.

"I didn't know it was you. You're a good fellow to trouble after me. I don't deserve it. I've been playing against you all this while, but I've lost. I staked my last chance to-night, but it wasn't any use; she's true as steel to you. I'm glad I've been able to tell you—you deserve her. I was a fool over my job. It's Rosa's doing this—curse her! I hope she'll get smashed up one of these days. He'll give her up then, like she did me. Yes, I hope she'll pay for this. I hope—"

The hand, raised as if to draw down a curse on the head of the wife who so little deserved the name, fell powerless to the seat, and the poor fellow was once more insensible.

There was no more Jerry could do for him, so he paid the cabman, who promised to see him safely to the hospital.

Carl Hermann and Lizette never met again.

The injuries he had received told upon an already shattered constitution. He lingered on for some few days, then died, alone and friendless; he who had once had his life bright and fair before him. The book was closed now, till the day when its soiled, crumpled pages should be known to all men.

Jerry stood for one or two moments on the scene of the accident after the cab and its senseless burden had driven away. Then suddenly he became aware that his peculiar appearance was causing the remainder of the crowd some amusement.

He woke from his dream with a queer smile, and set off at full speed to the circus tent, bounding over the few steps like one who walks "on" air.

The accident had been over in a few moments, but in a few more it would be time for him to take his turn with Lizette, for they were to go on together as usual.

He flung his coat into the dressing-room, and without staying to rearrange his dress, went once more to the ante-room.

It was full of people now, all asking where he was, all ready to surround him on his appearance. But he slipped unobserved to the farthest corner of the tent, where, waiting with a shade of fear on her face, was the little Fay of Fire. He stole softly to her side, and bent and kissed her softly.

She started, but he held both her hands in his, and looked down into her eyes; and, in spite of the paint and powder, she knew by his own grey ones that there was nothing now to fear—nothing to fear at all, but too much happiness.

" Where is the fellow? I do believe he'll be late," muttered one of the little group of performers gathered near.

Jerry smiled softly to himself. He knew he was not " too late " this time.

" Where are they? " cried Will Breakneck in great anger. " Where are they? "

" Here," said Jerry, unfastening Lizette's cloak, whispering as he did so,—" Come, little Liz, my wife that is to be; I'm ready; we go together, now, and always. Come."

And then, hand in hand, they began their life again.

And so we leave them, clown and rider,

IN THE RING.

THE END.

COLSTON AND COMPANY, PRINTERS, EDINBURGH.